All that love stuff people carried on about might be okay for others—but not for me,

Brad decided. He opened his bedroom door and abruptly halted. Rachel stood there, ready to knock.

"Uh, look, Rachel, I know I was way out of line earlier, and I apologize. I—"

She placed her fingers lightly across his lips. "I just came to tell you that if your offer is still open, I believe our getting married would solve a lot of problems."

Why hadn't she just taken a bat and hit him over the head? She couldn't have stunned him more.

"You want to marry me?"

Her smile was as sweet as an angel's. "I believe I do, Mr. Phillips. I believe I do."

Dear Reader,

June is busting out all over with this month's exciting lineup!

First up is Annette Broadrick's *But Not For Me.* We asked
Annette what kinds of stories she loved, and she admitted that a
heroine in love with her boss has always been one of her favorites.
In this romance, a reserved administrative assistant falls for her
sexy boss, but leaves her position when she receives threatening
letters. Well, this boss has another way to keep his beautiful
assistant by his side—marry her right away!

Royal Protocol by Christine Flynn is the next installment of the
CROWN AND GLORY series. Here, a lovely lady-in-waiting
teaches an admiral a thing or two about chemistry. Together, they
try to rescue royalty, but end up rescuing each other. And you can
never get enough of Susan Mallery's DESERT ROGUES series. In
The Prince & the Pregnant Princess, a headstrong woman finds
out she's pregnant with a seductive sheik's child. How long will it
take before she succumbs to his charms and his promise of happily
ever after?

In *The Last Wilder,* the fiery conclusion of Janis Reams Hudson's
WILDERS OF WYATT COUNTY, a willful heroine on a secret
quest winds up in a small town and locks horns with the handsome
local sheriff. Cheryl St.John's *Nick All Night* tells the story of a
down-on-her-luck woman who returns home and gets a second
chance at love with her very distracting next-door neighbor. In
Elizabeth Harbison's *Drive Me Wild,* a schoolbus-driving mom
struggles to make ends meet, but finds happiness with a former
flame who just happens to be her employer!

It's time to enjoy those lazy days of summer. So, grab a seat
by the pool and don't forget to bring your stack of emotional
tales of love, life and family from Silhouette Special Edition!

Sincerely,

Karen Taylor Richman
Senior Editor

Please address questions and book requests to:
Silhouette Reader Service
U.S.: 3010 Walden Ave., P.O. Box 1325, Buffalo, NY 14269
Canadian: P.O. Box 609, Fort Erie, Ont. L2A 5X3

Annette Broadrick

BUT NOT FOR ME

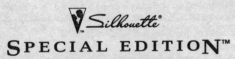

SPECIAL EDITION™

Published by Silhouette Books

America's Publisher of Contemporary Romance

To Patricia,
Who popped back into my life when I needed you the most.
You must be my fairy godmother!

Thank you for believing that I could write again. Your faith in
me has helped me regain my faith in myself. Here's to the next
twenty years together. Long may your magic wand wave.

  SILHOUETTE BOOKS

ISBN 0-373-24472-X

BUT NOT FOR ME

Visit Silhouette at www.eHarlequin.com

Printed in U.S.A.

Books by Annette Broadrick

ANNETTE BROADRICK

believes in romance and the magic of life. Since 1984, Annette has shared her view of life and love with readers. In addition to being nominated by *Romantic Times* as one of the Best New Authors of that year, she has also won the *Romantic Times* Reviewers' Choice Award for Best in its Series; the *Romantic Times* W.I.S.H. award; and the *Romantic Times* Lifetime Achievement Awards for Series Romance and Series Romantic Fantasy.

Chapter One

Where is she?

Brad Phillips slammed the phone back in its cradle. There had been no answer at Rachel Wood's home. Instead, all he'd heard was her cheerful recording inviting him to leave his name and number. She already knew his name and number. He was her boss and she should have been at work hours ago.

Impatient and more than a little unnerved by her continued absence, Brad shoved his chair away from his desk, stood and began to pace. He couldn't remember a time in the eight years she'd worked for him when Rachel hadn't called if she was running late.

So what is going on?

He glanced at his watch. Since she was generally

at her desk working hard by the time he arrived each morning around seven-thirty, that meant that she was more than two hours late.

The only scenario that made sense—and the thought scared the hell out of him—was that she'd been in an accident on her way to the office and was lying unconscious somewhere, unable to call him. Twice this morning he'd picked up the phone to call the various hospitals that served the metropolitan area of Dallas, Texas, to see if she had been taken to any of their emergency rooms.

So far, he'd managed to talk himself out of that move, at least for the time being. His head told him that it was too soon to panic. No doubt there was a perfectly logical explanation why she hadn't gotten in touch with him. Unfortunately for his peace of mind, he'd been unable to come up with one.

Brad continued to pace, wondering how long a person had to be missing before you could call the police. Probably more than two hours, which meant there was nothing he could do but wait, not his favorite form of activity. Or inactivity, which was why he'd never considered patience a virtue. He considered patience a complete waste of time.

His intercom rang and Brad almost leaped across the room to reach his desk.

"Yes?"

His secretary, Janelle, said, "I wanted to remind you of your ten o'clock meeting with Arthur Simmons."

"Thanks," he replied. He turned away from his

desk and walked over to the window. Just what he needed, he thought, his irritation and apprehension climbing another notch—a meeting with Arthur Simmons without Rachel to run interference.

The man was a genius with numbers and financial strategy. He'd saved Brad all kinds of money since he'd become the head of Phillips Construction Company's accounting department. Brad considered himself blessed to have the guy.

However, he dreaded each meeting that he was forced to sit through. Simmons had to be one of the most boring men Brad had ever encountered. Brad needed Rachel at the meeting as a buffer. She knew when he'd had enough of long-winded recitations delivered in an annoying monotone. She had a knack for bringing meetings to a close without offending anyone.

If Rachel didn't show up in the next fifteen minutes, Brad would be left on his own to suffer through Simmons's long-winded explanations of the latest reports from his department.

The numbers were essential to Brad and he would be the last person to deny their importance, but he would much prefer to look over the figures himself without having them explained to him in excruciating detail.

Maybe it was Simmons's attitude that bugged him. He came from a wealthy, upper-crust family somewhere back east. Arthur had made it clear during his interviews for the position that despite his moneyed background, he felt called to share his knowledge and expertise with humanity.

In Arthur's case, humanity appeared to be Phillips Construction Company, but Brad didn't care as long as Arthur continued to save—and therefore help to make—the company a great deal of money.

Although the two of them were close in age, he and Simmons couldn't be more different. Brad had come up the hard way. He was a street kid who had eventually built a multimillion-dollar construction business from little more than his back, his bare hands and encouragement from a man who had believed he had potential.

Simmons, on the other hand, had probably never worked up a sweat in his life. Instead, he had attended all the right private schools and graduated with honors from a prestigious eastern university.

Brad was in no way envious of the man. The gulf between their backgrounds just underlined the fact that they had nothing in common…except the mutual goal to make the company a success.

The way Brad saw it, he was a physical person. Simmons was a card-carrying intellectual. His carefully manicured hands made it obvious that Simmons had never picked up anything heavier than a pencil.

Brad turned away from the window, running his hand through his hair in agitation. He needed his invaluable administrative assistant and he needed her now.

He forced himself to return to his desk, almost

hearing Rachel's voice telling him to relax and use his time practicing patience.

Brad threw himself into his chair with a long-suffering sigh. Rachel's voice often echoed in his head. He figured she'd taken him on as some kind of project.

He would never forget the day he had hired her. He'd had no idea at the time that it was the smartest decision he'd ever make.

He'd been twenty-five, carefully tending a fledgling company by working long hours and generally sleeping in the construction trailer at his current building site.

He had a construction crew but no one who knew anything about the paperwork involved, including himself.

He'd been awarded the contract to build a multiplex theatre in north Dallas, the biggest job of his career. After the elation wore off, Brad had realized that he could no longer operate his growing business out of his apartment and a construction trailer.

He needed a bona fide office...with real office workers. He found the thought terrifying. An office would mean hiring—at the very least—a receptionist, a secretary and a bookkeeper. The latter job took up entirely too much of his time already.

The problem was that he couldn't afford to hire that many people. Not yet. But once he finished the multiplex, he felt that more business would come his way. He knew he provided quality structures. He'd worked hard to build a reputation for honesty, integrity and fair dealing.

Yes, there would be more work down the road, but until then he still worked on a shoestring budget.

Brad faced the reality of his situation and advertised for what he could afford—a receptionist—in the hope that whoever applied for the position might be able to do more than answer the phone.

His first step had been to lease office space. He'd negotiated the price with the owner by agreeing to do repair jobs on the building whenever needed. He'd worked on the new space every night and weekend.

When he placed the help-wanted ad in the paper, the office space was still a mess, which meant he had to figure out where to hold interviews. He couldn't expect a woman to show up at the project location and pick her way around building supplies, equipment and construction debris to get to his trailer. He eventually settled on a corner coffee shop near the site.

His phone rang repeatedly the day the ad first appeared. Brad was excited by the response. Surely he would find someone qualified within days.

A week later he was less excited. By then, he knew he was in deep trouble. Either the applicant wanted too much money or she didn't appear to know how to handle business calls or keep messages straight. By the third week, he was desperate.

Then Rachel Wood called.

"Phillips Construction," he yelled over the drilling noise going on outside.

In a cool, refined voice, she said, "Mr. Phillips, please."

Man, she sounded so professional that it never occurred to him she was anything but some CEO's administrative assistant.

"You've got him," he said grinning. He was already fantasizing about what the woman with the crisp—yet husky—voice might look like.

"I understand you're seeking a receptionist. Is the position still available?"

He'd been leaning back in his chair reading some reports when she called. At her words, he almost flipped over the chair. Struggling to maintain his balance, Brad triumphed over gravity enough to place his feet on the floor before saying, "Uh, yeah, uh, the position is open if you're interested." He heard the doubt in his voice and hoped she didn't notice.

She gave a quiet sigh that he could have sworn sounded like relief. But when she spoke her voice was perfectly composed.

"When may I set up an appointment to be interviewed?"

He almost told her the job was already hers if she wanted it, but managed to restrain himself. This must be some kind of mistake, but at least he'd get to see her in person and have his curiosity satisfied. With a person like her answering his phone, his office would immediately appear financially sound, stable, and trustworthy.

He was already lamenting the fact that he would never be able to afford to hire her.

He glanced at his watch. "Is it too late to meet today?" he asked and held his breath.

"Not at all. That would be fine. If you could give me your address and a time that would be convenient, I'll be there."

Now came the sticky part. "Well, the thing is, my office space won't be ready for occupancy until next week, but there's a coffee shop near my present project where we could meet, if that's okay with you—say around five o'clock?"

"Certainly," she replied with a crispness that he found attractive and calming.

He gave her the address and directions. After he hung up, he sat staring at the wall. *Don't get too excited,* he warned himself. *Once she finds out what a tiny operation this is and all the paperwork that keeping it running entails, a woman like her will laugh at the pittance of salary I have to offer.*

Brad forced his attention back to the reports before he returned to work with his crew. As the day progressed, he kept an eye on the clock to be certain he'd arrive at the interview on time.

By the time he walked into the coffee shop, Brad had washed up, but what he wore—faded jeans, a shirt with the sleeves ripped out and battered work boots covered with dust and grime—marked him for what he was: a construction worker. He might be the boss, but he knew he was too rough around the edges to mingle socially with the clientele he hoped to impress with his company's performance.

He glanced around the small café, realizing too late

that he'd neglected to get a description of Rachel Wood. He'd been more rattled at the time than he'd thought.

He rubbed his hand over his face, frowning. All right. Process of elimination. How many women were there? Alone?

Unfortunately, at least five.

Were any of them looking at him?

He dropped his head in disgust and stared at his boots. *All* of them watched him, and two of them wore predatory expressions.

A strong sense of relief coursed through him when a familiar voice from behind him said, "Pardon me, but are you Mr. Phillips?"

He turned and met the cool green gaze of a very attractive young woman who wore a tailored dress the color of her eyes. Her dark brown hair was pulled back in a knot and framed her heart-shaped face.

The top of her head was level with his chin.

"You must be Ms. Wood," he replied, a sense of relief that they'd connected washing over him. This woman couldn't actually save his life; it only felt that way.

She smiled and nodded. "I chose a booth toward the back, thinking it would be a little more private."

Brad almost missed what she said, because he was so intent on listening to her voice. In person, she sounded even more well-bred than she had on the phone. Rachel Wood was one classy lady. He was a little intimidated by her beauty, her poise and her obviously expensive education.

He wished he'd taken time to go to his apartment to change clothes, but it was too late now.

Brad motioned for her to lead the way and was treated to a view of her erect posture, her confident stride and a figure that was almost—but not quite—disguised by the prim dress she wore.

They sat across from each other. The waitress immediately appeared.

"Hi Brad," the waitress said, giving him the seductive smile that he'd seen every time she was on duty.

"Yeah, hi, Mitzi, just a cup of coffee, please."

Mitzi glanced at Rachel and motioned to the cup in front of her. "Need a refill?"

Rachel shook her head. "No, thank you."

Once the waitress left, Brad faced Rachel, wondering where to begin. He'd interviewed a dozen women so far, but today he felt like an awkward teenager on a first date. Either that, or as though he was the one being interviewed for a job he desperately wanted.

"I need to tell you up front that I have very little office experience," Rachel said, looking as though she'd confessed to a crime. "Your ad didn't state that you required experience, but I didn't want to mislead you."

"How are you at learning?" he asked, smiling. She was more nervous than he was, although she'd done a great job of disguising the fact. He relaxed a little, sat back and enjoyed the view. *She is one good-looking woman. Way above your league,* he reminded himself.

She gave a quick nod. "Show me what you want done and I'll do it."

Mitzi returned with his coffee. He nodded without taking his eyes off Rachel. "Thanks," he murmured. "You know anything about construction work?"

"No, sir."

He flinched in mock horror. "Hey, I'm not *that* much older than you. You don't need to 'sir' me." He noticed her hand trembling beside the coffee mug, confirming his assessment of her. She was nervous. Of him? Or the interview?

In an attempt to help her to relax, Brad described the company. "I formed my own company a little more than three years ago. I've worked construction since I was old enough to wear a tool belt and balance on a girder. What I don't know anything about is keeping up with bills and payroll and the kind of paperwork that IRS insists I file on a regular basis."

She picked up her cup and delicately sipped before she commented. "Your ad said something about being a receptionist," she said with a hint of question in her voice.

"Yeah, because once I have the office open, I need someone to handle calls. I lose more business than I want to think about because I'm unable to check my answering machine at home more often. I get involved in a project and forget about everything else, but I know I can't keep doing that or I'll lose the momentum I've got going for me."

"Yes, I can understand that," she said slowly. She paused, as though searching for words. Finally she said, "About the salary—" she began, then stopped when he waved his hand as though a salary was incidental.

He knew this was the tricky part. He'd lose her when she heard what the job paid. He had to pitch the job as one of opportunity for greater things in the future. His con-artist dad had given Brad innumerable examples of how to convince a mark the future looked rosy.

"The thing is," he said with what he hoped was a confident grin, "I'm getting more business than I can handle without working around the clock, which is close to what I'm doing already. The jobs are there, you see, but right now my cash flow is a little tight. If you're willing to work for me, we can work something out now for a starting salary with a firm promise that your pay will increase steadily as we grow."

Although her shoulders remained the same, Brad got the impression that Rachel had slumped into the bench at his explanation.

He sighed. "How much money were you looking for?" he asked, almost holding his breath for the answer.

"I don't have a set figure. I finished college in May. I need to find work. My mother has some health problems and can no longer work. She sacrificed a comfortable life to ensure that my brother, sister and I received a good education. I don't want her to worry about money. She's done enough." She sounded composed. Only the pain in her eyes revealed her emotions.

"Are you saying you've never worked before?" he asked, rubbing his cheek and realizing he should have shaved before the meeting.

Her lips curled into a wry smile. "Oh, I've worked, Mr. Phillips. Just not in an office. I began baby-sitting when I was thirteen, bused tables during high school and graduated to waitress in college. So yes, I've worked before," she quietly added.

He tried not to let his astonishment show. If he'd been asked to guess, he would have said that Rachel Wood had been born with a silver spoon in her mouth and had never needed to lift her hand to any sort of menial labor.

"Where did you go to school?" he asked, his curiosity aroused.

"Southern Methodist University. I wanted to stay close to home and was fortunate to receive a scholastic scholarship that helped me do so."

"You've got me beat by a long shot. I managed an education of sorts, mostly by going to night school while I worked during the day." As soon as he stopped speaking, Brad was appalled that he had mentioned his background to her. He never discussed his past. Talk about sabotaging himself! He quickly continued. "What did you major in?"

Her smile flashed once more. "You might find it strange for me to interview for a receptionist position, but I took all the business courses I could...accounting, business law, office management..."

She continued to list the subjects he knew little

about. He had to pinch himself to be sure he wasn't dreaming. When she finished her list, he said, "I'll make a deal with you."

"Go on."

"If you'll come to work for me starting next Monday, you can decide your salary. Look at the books and the overhead. Pay yourself whatever's left. How's that?"

"You can't be serious." Disapproval frosted her words. He wasn't surprised. Her reaction was proof enough he'd chosen the perfect candidate for the job.

"I need someone with your skills," he said, wanting to convince her he wasn't a complete loon. "Do you intend to take advantage of me?"

She looked at him with reproach. "Of course not."

"Then I don't see a problem."

"I've never heard of such a thing." She eyed him for the first time with suspicion.

He grinned. "Yeah, I know what you're thinking, but no, I don't do drugs and outside of an occasional beer, don't drink much, either."

"How did you know what I was thinking?" she asked, startled.

"You have a very expressive face," he replied, still smiling. "So, will you consider it? I can take you to the office. I still have a lot to do to have it ready by Monday, but I promise you a place to work by then." He paused, silently pleading for her to agree.

"All right," she eventually said, sounding a little uncertain.

"Great," he said, immediately standing. "You want to ride with me?"

She moved more slowly and with a great deal more grace. "It would be more efficient if I followed you, wouldn't it?"

Already thinking ahead, he thought, barely able to control the grin that kept threatening to break out. "Sure. Whatever you want." He left a tip on the table, stopped and paid for their coffee and escorted her outside. "Where's your car?"

She pointed to a small economy car that looked well used and equally well cared for.

"I'm over here," he said, pointing to his beat-up truck with its faded red finish that blended well with the rust. After escorting her to her car, he strode to his truck and got in. He waited until she pulled out before he moved into traffic.

Brad was excited about being able to show off his office to someone. He'd been working out of his small apartment so long that he could barely find his way through the place, what with all the papers, files and other business-related products scattered around.

He drove to an older part of town and pulled into the parking lot of a red-brick building from the 1930s. Someday he'd have his own building or a large suite of offices in a prestigious office complex.

Brad stood by his truck and waited for Ms. Wood to pull into the space next to him. Three parking spaces were marked with signs saying Reserved for Phillips Construction Company.

Here was physical proof that he had moved up in

the business world. With Ms. Wood's help, there would be no stopping the company's growth.

Of course, the future wasn't reflected in his account ledgers just yet, but he knew the money would be there in the next few years.

They took the elevator to the third floor without speaking. The office was on the top floor, with a nice view of downtown Dallas.

He walked to the end of the hall and unlocked the door with a frosted-glass window. With a slight bow, he stepped back and waved her through the open doorway.

She stepped into the newly renovated space and stopped. "Oh, my. I wasn't expecting anything quite this large."

He shrugged. "Well, I figured that since I'm going to be here for a while I'd take the space while it was available. Besides, there will be offices for my site supervisors—when I get them—and I'll need an office, as will you. Eventually there needs to be a place for a receptionist—"

She turned and faced him with raised brows. "I thought *I* was going to be your receptionist?"

He nodded. "Sure, at first. But the way I see it, some day you'll be my administrative assistant with a secretary of your own. That is, if you want to invest your time and energy into making all of this work."

She walked to one of the windows and looked out. The two men he'd pulled off his crew to finish the place had left everything where they'd been working at quitting time, thinking no one would see the mess.

Brad was so used to the clutter of renovation that he'd been oblivious to the mess until now. Seeing the place through her eyes, he could understand that she might not be quite as impressed as he'd hoped.

When she turned away from the window, she looked around at the large open space, her brows raised slightly. "Are you sure this will be finished by Monday? That's less than a week away."

"No problem. We'll finish a few rooms now and leave the rest of the area for storage. Since none of my clients ever see my office, there's no reason to get fancy."

She nodded thoughtfully as she continued to inspect the space.

He waited, not wanting to push her. He'd given her the best pitch he could. The decision was hers. He wished there was some way he could show her his vision for the company. There were no guarantees, of course, but he knew that hard work could produce amazing results.

Brad watched while she stepped over and around the clutter and studied the layout from a drawing pinned to one of the walls. Without turning, she asked, "I'm presuming that you'll have furniture?"

He laughed. "It'll be delivered Monday. It's used but in good shape."

She continued to prowl until she'd seen everything. Rachel walked to where he stood and asked, "What time do you want me here on Monday?"

He breathed a sigh of relief, knowing the company was on its way.

Since then they'd been a team. They had worked together smoothly and efficiently for eight years. He had a hunch that was due more to her diplomacy than to his communication skills. Once he got to know her, Brad discovered Rachel to be as conservative and well-bred as she had appeared to be at the interview. She had a strong work ethic, which he appreciated.

Rachel worked every day for years, through blistering heat waves, drenching downpours, occasional winter sleet storms and once when she'd had the flu.

So where was she today?

Brad didn't want to contemplate what would happen if Rachel weren't there to help him run the company. She'd taken on the administrative side of things, leaving him free to do what he did best, build commercial projects.

Within three years, they'd hired more people, including Janelle. Before long, Accounting needed a leader—so he'd hired Arthur. Eventually Rich Harmon took the helm as office manager.

Rachel continued to amaze him. She accompanied him to business dinners with potential clients. She rarely spoke, and if the visitors thought she was there as arm candy, their assumption gave him an advantage. Rachel had a gift—she was a wizard at interpreting expressions, body language and what was implied but not said.

Later, she gave him her impressions of the people and how best to provide what they wanted. Together they would work out proposals with the added data she'd provided. Within a couple of years, Rachel had become more of a partner in the business than a mere assistant. He brought up the idea of making her a partner on more than one occasion. She had refused to discuss the matter with him.

Their present relationship disturbed him not only because she would not accept the partnership she deserved, but because of his attraction to her.

Brad disliked the thought that he was taking advantage of her. She was his business equal, but they both knew he was nowhere near her social equal.

He had never acted on his initial attraction to her. The fear that she might leave the company if he suggested they date had kept him from doing or saying anything that might offend her.

Several weeks ago, they had dinner together to celebrate another first for Phillips Construction Company—their first out-of-state job.

Not only was the new project not in Texas, it wasn't a commercial building—another first. One of his clients had asked him to bid on a second home for him and his wife to be built in the mountains near Asheville, North Carolina.

Brad ignored the dire predictions of Carl Jackson, his senior supervisor and project manager. Carl pointed out to Brad that constructing a residence was considerably different from building commercial projects. Generally speaking, the project manager had to deal with a wife, which could be a real pain.

Brad had laughed and told him that he had the experience to cope. Carl had not been amused, but he'd taken the assignment, as Brad had known he would.

Carl had been invited to join the dinner celebration but had declined, saying the time to celebrate would be after the project was completed.

Brad and Rachel didn't see it that way. They were too excited about another avenue opening up for the company. They'd reminisced over their salads, entrées, desserts and coffee about the years they'd worked together, recounting stories to each other. The evening lingered in his memory. He'd been light-hearted and filled with a buoyancy that occurred when he was around Rachel.

Rachel Wood was his best friend. Actually, she was his only friend. He didn't have time to socialize. He felt comfortable with her. In addition, he trusted her. He trusted few people.

Where was she this morning?

His thoughts were interrupted by the sound of the intercom. He blinked, wondering how long he'd been daydreaming.

"Yes?" he asked. Then he knew exactly how long he'd been lost in his thoughts when Janelle said, "Mr. Simmons is here."

"Thanks," he said, heroically not groaning in her ear. "Have him come in."

Brad straightened in his chair and prepared himself for another boring meeting.

Simmons stepped silently into the room and quietly closed the door behind him. He looked around the room.

"Isn't Ms. Wood going to be here?" he asked, not

bothering to hide his dismay at the prospect of dealing with Brad on his own.

Brad could certainly sympathize with Arthur's obvious discomfort. "She's been detained for some reason," he replied briskly. "I'm certain we can manage to struggle through your reports without her."

Simmons sat in one of the padded chairs in front of Brad's desk. He placed a stack of folders precisely in front of him and pushed his wire-rimmed eyeglasses to the bridge of his nose, where they promptly slid to their original resting place.

He cleared his throat unhappily. "I was hoping that Ms. Wood would be able to—" he began before Brad interrupted.

"So was I, but she's not here. So let's get on with it."

Simmons flinched and Brad silently cursed. *Rachel,* he thought, *you'd better have a darned good reason for leaving me alone with Arthur. Otherwise I'll make you pay for this—big time.*

Forty-five minutes later, just as Brad's eyes had begun to roll to the back of his head, his prayers were answered. Rachel opened the door to his office, looking as she always did, impeccably dressed and carrying a briefcase—the epitome of the modern businesswoman.

It was all Brad could do not to throw himself at her feet and beg her never to desert him like this again.

Now that he knew she was safe, he felt the beginnings of irritation seep into his consciousness.

Couldn't she have called? If she hadn't intended to be here at the usual time, was there any reason why she couldn't have shown him the courtesy of advising him of that fact?

He met her eyes and realized that whatever had delayed her wasn't good. He couldn't remember ever seeing her look so fragile. She had the same stricken look she'd worn when she'd gotten the news that her mother was terminally ill.

What in the world had happened?

Rachel walked to the desk, took the chair next to Arthur and gracefully seated herself.

"I apologize for my tardiness, gentlemen," she said calmly. "Now then, where are we?" she asked, picking up the stack of papers that Simmons had placed in front of her chair earlier.

By the time the meeting was finally over, Brad's jaw hurt from clenching his teeth. Rachel walked Simmons to the door, spoke a few—no doubt kind—words to him and smiled at his almost inaudible response.

She closed the door behind him and turned to Brad. "I apologize for coming into work so late and for not calling to let you know." She walked back to her chair and sat before she continued. "I need to take a leave of absence, Brad. If that's not convenient for you, I certainly can understand that you might wish to replace me."

Chapter Two

Brad stared at her in shock...glad he was seated. Otherwise he would have made a fool of himself when his knees gave way at her calm announcement.

Rachel had just verbalized his greatest fear, only he hadn't known it until now. The constriction in his chest made it difficult for him to breathe. He wondered if he were having a heart attack.

She sat there, waiting for him to say something.

His mind was blank. She intended to take a leave of absence? When he'd had trouble getting through a morning without her?

Then it hit him. She was kidding! "All right," he said with a grin, "what is this? Are you hitting me up for another raise? If so, consider yourself successful."

Rachel leaned forward in her chair. "I know this comes as a shock to you, Brad, and I'm sorry if my being away is going to inconvenience you. After seriously considering all of my options, I believe my getting away for a while will be best for all concerned."

She wasn't kidding.

He swallowed hard, hanging on to his control so that he didn't pound the desk and bellow at her. Not that she hadn't witnessed some of that behavior over the years, but it had never been aimed at her. Desolation swept over him at the idea that Rachel could so casually walk away from the business she had helped to create.

"Do I have any say in your decision or is it already written in stone?" he asked mildly. Only his clenched hands resting on the desk gave away his agitation. If she happened to notice.

Rachel sighed and looked toward the window for a long moment before turning back to him. "I haven't wanted to bother you with any of this," she finally said.

"Too late. I'm bothered. Now, what the hell is going on, Rachel?"

She leaned back in her chair and gave him a level stare. "Would it help if I told you it is personal and has nothing to do with the business?"

"I'm glad to hear it. Now tell me what's going on."

"You're going to be difficult about this, aren't you?" she asked, frowning.

He leaned forward. "You have no idea how difficult I'm going to be if you don't start explaining—now—what has happened." He enunciated each word with utmost precision.

Rachel sat up, clasping her hands tightly on the desk. "A few weeks ago I found an anonymous note in my apartment building mailbox. I'd never had anything like that happen to me before."

"What did it say?"

"I don't remember exactly. It was signed 'Your Secret Admirer.' The notes didn't bother me at first—"

"Notes? You received more than one?"

She nodded. "They arrived every week or so and said things like 'I'm so glad I know you…I want to spend time with you'…that sort of thing. As time passed the notes became more…more…personal." She flushed. "They stated how much the writer wanted to hold me, kiss me…and…um…"

Brad could see she was uncomfortable discussing the matter with him.

"I threw the notes away as soon as I found them. I tried to ignore them because I knew there was nothing I could do. The police said the same thing."

Brad froze. "The police?"

"Yes. That's where I've been this morning…talking with the police."

Brad didn't like what he was hearing. She'd been receiving anonymous notes that had caused her to report them to the police and had never mentioned them to him. He wondered why? Did she truly see him as no more than her boss?

"What happened that made you go to the police?"

She bit her bottom lip and he realized she was trembling. "I arrived home late last night and immediately went to bed. This morning I took my shower and dressed as I usually do. When I went to my dresser to pick out a pair of earrings, I noticed there was a folded note lying on top of the dresser. I don't know how long it had been there."

Brad almost came out of his chair in outrage but knew he had to hang on to his temper until she told him the details. It took real effort for him to remain calm while he listened to her.

"At first I thought it was from my cleaning lady—she'd been there the day before—but she generally leaves a message by the kitchen phone. When I opened it, I saw it was signed 'Your Secret Admirer.'"

Rachel had been looking at her hands during her recital. Now she looked up at him. She looked terrified. She struggled to sound calm as she said, "Whoever this is was inside my apartment either yesterday or last night. I immediately called my cleaning lady, but she said she hadn't seen anyone. As I told the police, whoever wrote it could have placed it there while I was asleep for all I know." She covered her eyes for a moment, then went on. "I panicked when I saw the note. For a moment I even imagined he was still there, lurking in my closet, but then I remembered I would have seen him when I got dressed. All

I knew was I had to get out of the apartment. So I went to the police.''

Brad went back to her earlier statement. ''They told you there is nothing they can do?''

''Basically. After waiting for over an hour to speak to someone, I told the man on duty what happened. He listened, asked questions and typed up the report. I gave him the note I'd found, the only one I'd kept. He asked if I'd recently broken up with a boyfriend who might have a key to my place! I was upset by the suggestion. I told him no, of course. He said that even though the note suggested someone had unlawfully entered my apartment, they didn't have the manpower to check out this kind of complaint. He suggested I might want to leave town for a while.''

''This is why you intend to take a leave of absence?''

She nodded. ''I don't think I can sleep there again, knowing that someone can get into the apartment without my knowledge. I thought I'd take some time off and decide what to do. It's not that I haven't enjoyed working here, but until I've come up with some kind of resolution for this matter, I don't think I'd be much use to the company.''

Now it was Brad's turn to panic. There was no way he was going to let her walk out of here and go who knows where. He'd be worried sick about her. What if the guy followed her? She still wouldn't be safe.

Thinking furiously, Brad said, ''I can certainly understand your concerns, Rachel,'' he began. ''I believe if we sit down together and assess what has happened, we can—'' The intercom interrupted him.

Not bothering to hide his irritation at the interruption, he punched the button and growled, ''Yes?''

''Sorry to interrupt,'' were Janelle's first words. ''Carl is on line three and says he needs to talk to you now. What would you like me to tell him?''

''I'll take it,'' he said with resignation. Business continued despite the bombshell Rachel had dropped on him.

Hitting the button for the speakerphone, he said, ''Hey, buddy, how's it going?''

''I'm ready to turn in my resignation on this one, Brad. I've just about had it!''

Brad glanced at Rachel. ''There seems to be a lot of that going around these days. What's up?''

''Thomas Crossland's wife turned up at the site two weeks ago and has taken responsibility for overseeing the construction of their home. She's made it clear that she is not pleased with what's being done. Today she informed me that she wanted an immediate meeting with you—on-site, mind you—for a full explanation of why we continue to ignore her many suggestions to improve her home.''

''Where's Tom?''

''Who knows? Hell, he's probably gone into hiding until the house is finished. Look, I know how much you wanted the opportunity to expand our market, but I'm telling you right now, if we manage to get through this project without being sued or losing our shirts over her costly proposed changes, I'll consider us way ahead of the game.''

Carl had been with him since the beginning, and Brad learned a long time ago to listen to him. If he said the situation was serious, Brad believed him. Hearing the testiness in Carl's voice, Brad deliberately used a light tone when he replied, ''That bad, huh?''

''Worse,'' Carl snapped back. ''When can you get here?''

Brad hadn't taken his eyes off Rachel during the conversation. His brain kicked into high gear. Maybe this could be used to his advantage. He did not want to lose Rachel, even for a few days, much less weeks or months.

He mentally reviewed his schedule and realized that nothing had gone according to plan since he had arrived that morning to discover Rachel was missing. He scanned his appointment book, then answered Carl.

''I should be able to be in Asheville by five or thereabout.''

Carl gave a sigh of relief. ''Great. I'll be there to meet you. We're about forty miles from Asheville. I can fill you in on the particulars on our way back.''

''Sounds good to me. Oh, and Carl?''

''Yeah?'' Carl sounded much better already.

''Take the rest of the day off...boss's orders.''

Carl's rumbling laugh filled the room, causing Rachel to smile. ''You don't have to say that twice. See ya around five,'' he replied and hung up.

Brad broke the connection, then hit the speed dial. When a voice answered, he asked, "Steve, how soon can you have the plane ready?"

Without hesitation, Steve Parsons, the pilot of the company's jet, replied, "Within the hour. Where are we going?"

"Asheville, North Carolina. Rachel and I will grab a quick bite to eat and see you at the hangar." He hung up without looking at her and waited.

He didn't have to wait long.

"I can't go to North Carolina with you, Brad! I need to pack to leave town as soon as possible. I thought I made that clear to you."

Brad smiled and spread his arms in an expansive movement. "Don't you see? That's exactly what you're doing. I think Carl has inadvertently come up with the perfect solution. You can leave town and continue to work."

Her exasperation with him almost made him laugh. He felt better already. He was buying time until he could think of something else. She'd sprung this on him today, while she had been dealing with it for some time.

"Going to North Carolina is a temporary fix, Brad." She sounded as though she were attempting to reason with an obstinate child.

He nodded, feeling better the more he thought about his impromptu plan. "Of course it's temporary, but the trip will give us time to look at other options that don't include your taking a leave of absence," he replied, using the same reasoning tone of voice.

"I've already gone over the options." She was beginning to sound downright testy. "This is the best one."

"How do you know? Maybe I'll think of something you haven't considered. What do you have to lose?"

She shook her head. "It's just postponing the inevitable, Brad, and you know it."

"Humor me, all right?" He stood and walked around the desk. "Let's go find something to eat before we head to the airport."

"I can't go with you without advance notice. I need some clothes. I—"

"You can buy anything you need there. Let's go." He picked up his briefcase, which always carried a fresh shirt, underwear and socks—but he saw no reason to apprise her of that fact—and on impulse grabbed her hand to assist her out of her chair. The unexpected contact startled them both.

From the day he had hired her, Brad had deliberately refrained from physical contact with Rachel. He'd decided that keeping her at a safe distance would be the wisest course of action.

Rachel stood and immediately removed her hand from his. She made it obvious that she was not pleased with his solution. "This isn't a good idea, you know," she argued valiantly, but she knew him well enough by now to know he wouldn't give in.

"On the contrary," he replied with a grin. "I'm convinced I've come up with a brilliant piece of strategy. C'mon, let's get something to eat. I'm starving."

She followed him through his office door, no doubt continuing to marshal her arguments, he thought.

He stopped at his secretary's desk. "Janelle, cancel any appointments Rachel and I have for the rest of the week." He looked at his watch and grimaced. "Rich is no doubt somewhere having lunch."

Richard Harmon had taken on the onerous task of office manager five years ago. He had excellent skills for keeping the place running smoothly. Since Brad and Rachel were seldom gone at the same time, Brad had never had to rely on Rich's ability to take over the reins of the company. This might be an excellent opportunity to see how well he handled the responsibility.

"Please send a memo to Rich and tell him we'll both be out of town for the next few days and that he's in charge. If he needs to contact me, I'll have my cell phone with me. Be sure to give him that number. If anything comes up that he doesn't feel qualified to handle, tell him I want him to contact me immediately." Janelle wrote the instructions down, keeping up with him with seeming ease.

Janelle Andrews had come to work for the company five years ago as well. In her late forties, Janelle was a human dynamo, keeping up with the paperwork for both of them without showing stress or strain. Brad appreciated the fact that Janelle did not gossip, kept her work confidential and had a pleasant disposition. He knew he'd been fortunate to gather together such a solid, dependable staff.

Janelle quickly scanned the appointment book, reminding him of what appointments were being canceled. He suggested that she reschedule all of them for early next week. "Explain that an emergency called me out of town," he concluded.

She smiled and said, "Have a safe trip," including both of them in the statement.

Brad turned, and he and Rachel followed the hallway into the large reception area. Melinda, the young receptionist, smiled at them. Brad nodded and walked toward the company's entrance—double glass doors bearing the inscription Phillips Construction Company.

Brad mentally ran through what Rachel had told him—while they waited for the elevator, rode down to the basement parking garage and walked to his sleek sports car.

There were times when Rachel irritated him with her insistence on being so blasted self-sufficient. On the other hand, that's what made her such a great assistant.

Rachel broke the silence between them when they reached his car. "You don't have to do this, you know," she said, sounding almost reconciled to the trip, which made her continued resistance to his plan easier on him. She glanced at him while he held the door open on the passenger's side. She slid into the low car with more grace than most women he knew, but then Rachel had always had an air of refinement about her.

Over the years she'd worked for him, she had managed to polish some of his rough edges without making him feel boorish or embarrassed by his lack of sophistication.

He felt justified in offering his help now, despite her protests.

Brad slid behind the steering wheel, closed the car door and started the engine, which began to purr like a well-fed cat. He smiled. Before owning this particular vehicle, Brad had bought only trucks for his own use. They were by far the most practical transportation for business purposes.

For years after he knew he could afford to drive anything he wished, he continued to drive a pickup truck...until he'd seen this baby sitting in a show window three months ago. Practicality took a back seat to the sleek lines and high performance of the Porsche. He'd never had buyer's remorse; he doubted very much that he ever would.

The car was a visible sign that he'd met his goals and become successful. His success meant he had overcome his early life. His past no longer had the power to cause him pain, because he had proven to himself that he wasn't a loser. His new Porsche reminded him that he was a winner every time he saw it.

Rachel forced herself to lean back in the aircraft seat. She closed her eyes, already dreading the petrifying moment when the jet actually left Mother Earth and threw itself recklessly into the air, defying the law of gravity.

She did not like to fly. To be more precise, she

absolutely *detested* flying and generally managed to avoid it, but there was no arguing with Brad.

Not that Brad had any idea of her strong aversion to flying. She'd been careful never to mention the matter to him. After all, there had never been a reason to call his attention to her weakness. Sometime during the years she had worked for him, Brad must have decided that she was a direct descendant of Wonder Woman—he thought that no matter what he asked of her, she could do it with ease.

Boy, was he wrong. For whatever reason—and she had no doubt an analyst would have a field day with this one—she had worked diligently to keep Brad's illusions about her intact.

Until now. All she wanted to do at the moment was curl up somewhere and sleep for the next year or so. After what had happened last night, though, she no longer felt safe in her apartment.

Rachel gripped the arms of her seat as the plane barreled down the runway and leaped skyward. She prayed fervently that she wouldn't embarrass herself by becoming hysterical and sobbing all the way to North Carolina.

Even with her eyes closed, she knew when Brad unfastened his safety belt and left the seat beside her. The company jet contained a fully equipped office. Wherever Brad went, he kept up with everything that happened in his company.

She kept her eyes closed in order to better concentrate on the sounds of the plane. Perhaps if she re-

mained alert, she could warn Steve if a wing fell off
or something.

She hoped Brad would be able to deal satisfactorily
with Mrs. Crossland. He'd been so excited when
Thomas Crossland asked him to build his vacation
home in the mountains.

There was no reason for Carl to worry. Brad had
an excellent track record for convincing a person that
Brad's way was the best way. Her being there on the
plane with him certainly proved his powers of per-
suasion. He'd used them successfully on other occasions.

He'd convinced her years ago that helping him
build his dream company would not only bring her
wealth but also tremendous satisfaction.

What normal, red-blooded woman wouldn't have
fallen in love with him?

Of course she'd never, by look or deed, revealed
her feelings to him. Not only would that have sabo-
taged her career, but it would also have sent Brad
Phillips running for the nearest exit.

She almost smiled at that thought but, if Brad happened to notice that she wasn't asleep, he'd want to
continue to discuss her plan to take some time off.
She wasn't ready to go another round with him on
that subject.

Rachel seldom discussed her private life with Brad.
One of the ways she avoided personal topics was to
turn his casual questions around to find out about *his*
social life. Over the years he'd been surprisingly
forthcoming about who he was seeing and who he

had stopped seeing. Rachel wasn't sure which was worse, imagining Brad with various women or actually hearing about them.

She'd formed a clear picture of his modus operandi in the romance department. There wasn't an ounce of romance in the man, which was really a shame because he was the type of male that women fantasized about while gnawing on a knuckle and whimpering.

Working construction had honed his tall, rangy body into solid muscle and sinew. Along the way he'd acquired what appeared to be a permanent tan as a result of years spent working in the sun. She wasn't sure how he managed to keep his trim good looks now that he spent a large part of his time indoors, but there was no doubt a hard body lurked beneath his custom-made suits.

As one of her friends so succinctly put it, if she *hadn't* fallen in love with the man after working closely with him for years, someone would have needed to check her pulse to be certain she was alive.

He had no trouble attracting the attention of women, married or single, but the man appeared uninterested in their admiration. She couldn't say he was classically handsome…his face showed too much strength for that. How he remained unaware of his ability to charm any woman he wanted into his bed was beyond her. Having known other men who used that particular skill to seduce women who could put them in touch with business contacts, she knew that Brad was an exceptional man. He never used his sensual appeal as a manipulative tool.

Rachel knew that he sometimes dated daughters of leading businessmen in Dallas, not because he ever mentioned them, but because he was frequently seen in photographs prominently displayed on the society pages of the daily newspaper. She knew when he'd stopped seeing one of them by the stack of phone messages he received, pleading with him to call.

She recalled one night about a year after she had gone to work for him. They had worked late at the office. As usual Brad had offered to feed her. Once they had eaten and he was in a relaxed mood, he surprised her by mentioning a couple of the women he'd been seeing, giving her new insight into his complicated thought processes.

They had been enjoying their after-dinner coffee when in a rare burst of curiosity, she asked, "I noticed that Caroline Windsor has been calling frequently during the past few days. Is there a problem with your relationship?"

He winced, making her wish she could cut off her tongue before it got her into any more trouble. "The problem is that she thinks we *have* a relationship," he replied gruffly.

He must have registered her surprise at his comment because he continued in explanation. "You see, Caroline always gets whatever she wants that daddy can buy, which covers a lot of territory, given Carter Windsor the Third's bank balance. She kept turning up whenever her dad and I met while planning his latest commercial venture, joining us for lunch and suggesting not too subtly that she was available for dinner.''

He sipped on his coffee and Rachel hoped he would continue with this story, because it sounded like a good one. There weren't too many—all right, if she were being honest—she didn't know of *any* man who wouldn't be flattered by drawing Ms. Windsor's attention, giving him an opportunity to get in closer touch with the Carter Windsor dynasty.

She kept her gaze on her coffee, not wanting to let him see how his remarks had only whetted her no-doubt morbid curiosity concerning his love life.

''I'm not making excuses in regard to my behavior,'' he said after a long pause. ''CeCe is attractive, intelligent and never boring. What she can be at times is demanding. She doesn't like the hours I work because she's used to having an escort at her beck and call. When I explained that she was free to find someone else since I couldn't always meet her requirements, she resorted to tears and said things I know she regrets. I realized that if she pictured us as a couple headed toward commitment, I had to step out of her life immediately. So I did.'' The firm tone he used indicated that he'd made up his mind. ''I'm not sure she believed me.''

''Hence her telephone calls?'' Rachel asked with a slight smile.

He shrugged. ''I guess. She discovered that I don't play games when she hoped to punish me by not being available when I found time to call. I suppose she

wanted to make me jealous.'' His smile was rueful.
''That doesn't work with me.''

''So you aren't looking for a long-term commitment, I take it?'' she asked very casually.

''I already have one,'' he replied, settling comfortably back into the plush banquette.

Rachel hoped she'd covered her startled reaction.
She couldn't think of anyone who had been in his life
for more than a few months since he'd hired her. ''I
see,'' she said. ''Have I met her?''

He grinned. ''It's not a her. It's this business, Rachel. I thought you of all people would understand
that.''

''Ah,'' she replied, feeling a strong sense of relief
that he hadn't been referring to another woman,
which was stupid of her. What difference could it
make to her?

''I learned a long time ago,'' he continued, ''that
relationships never work out in the long run. Besides,
they take too much time and energy. Most women I
know are looking for a husband and a father for their
future children. Since I'm not going to be either of
those things, I rarely stay with one woman for more
than a few months.''

As the plane winged eastward, Rachel remembered
everything he'd said that night. She'd been relieved
in a way that she wouldn't have to witness her boss
someday marrying some blushing bride. However, his
remarks had also made her wonder why he was so
certain he would never marry. She may have been
given a glimpse of his fiercely guarded past a few

years ago. Janelle had forwarded one of Brad's calls to her when he was out of town.

"This is Rachel Wood, Mr. Phillips' assistant. May I help you?"

"Not unless you happen to be sitting on Brad's lap. I want to speak to my son and I intend to speak to my son. So put him on the line. Now."

Brad never mentioned his family. She had somehow received the impression that his parents were dead. Obviously she'd been wrong.

"I'm sorry, Mr. Phillips," she said, her voice warming, "Brad is out of town. He won't be back until the end of the week. Would you like me to give him a message?"

She heard a distinct growl of displeasure before the man said, "Why don't you do that? Why don't you ask him why he never returns my phone calls? Why don't you ask him why he looked through me as though I didn't exist when he left some muckymuck's posh party at the Marriott Hotel last week? And ask him why he refuses to meet me, completely ignoring all the years I spent raising him?"

More hesitant now, she answered, "Yes, Mr. Phillips, I'll give him the message."

"And tell him I expect to hear from him as soon as he returns to town."

"I will," she said quietly.

"Oh, and for the record—my name isn't Phillips. It's Harold Freeland." He slammed the phone down, causing her to wince.

She'd carefully recorded everything the man had

said in a memo and placed it in the center of Brad's desk so that he would see it as soon as he returned. The first time she entered Brad's office after his return she saw the typed message crumpled in his wastebasket.

Neither of them mentioned the phone call or the message she'd relayed to him. She'd never felt it was any of her business to ask questions about his parents and Brad certainly hadn't volunteered any explanations.

He'd been raised by his father? What had happened to his mother? Did his relationship with his parents have anything to do with his strongly held desire not to marry?

Who knew?

That phone call was the only time she'd been shown a glimpse of his life before she'd gone to work for him. She had a hunch she might understand Brad better if he were willing to discuss his childhood with her, but he never mentioned it.

On the other hand, he'd been wonderfully compassionate when her mother had been diagnosed as terminally ill. He'd told Rachel to stay home with her mother after the surgery that had confirmed the diagnosis, and he'd continued to pay her salary despite her protests. In addition, he'd paid off the medical bills that weren't covered by her mother's insurance. Rachel had been heartbroken that she'd been home with her mother for only a few weeks before she succumbed to her illness.

Rachel had been the one to deal with the arrangements, which was only fair. Both her brother and his family and her sister, who was single, lived in California. Rachel was the one who had stayed home with her mother for all those years.

She'd lost her mother four years ago and Rachel still missed her. She'd had a rough time adjusting to the loss. Brad had been more than supportive.

So he had a heart. He just didn't want the knowledge to get around. The news might ruin his reputation for being a tough, hardheaded businessman.

"Rachel?"

Startled, Rachel sat up, opening her eyes. "Yes?" she said, her voice hoarse.

He grinned. "No, we're not crashing, so you can relax, if that's possible."

She frowned. "What are you talking about?"

"Somehow I've managed to get the impression during this trip that you're afraid of flying."

Wouldn't you know his powers of observation would zero in on something like that when he was oblivious to so many other things, Rachel thought, irritated. Maybe she could bluff him.

"I don't know where you got the idea that I'm afraid of flying," she replied with as much dignity as she could muster.

He raised one of his brows in feigned surprise. "You don't say," he drawled, looking amused. "You were clutching the arms of your seat so hard when we took off that you actually left permanent dents where your fingernails dug into the leather."

She quickly checked the arms to make sure she

hadn't done that very thing when his laughter made her realize she'd given herself away.

"I don't fly very often," she admitted, still trying to hang on to her dignity, which appeared to be slipping rapidly away.

"Oh, I'm well aware of that. I'm also aware how close you were to mutiny when we boarded."

"That's because there is no good reason for me to be on this trip," she replied, feeling defensive.

"I can think of several off the top of my head but this isn't the time to go into them."

She stared wildly around the cabin and tightly gripped the arms of her seat. "Why?" she demanded.

He gave her that lopsided grin of his—the one that usually melted her heart no matter how aggravated she might be with him—and said, "Captain says we'll be landing in another thirty minutes or so. Thought you'd want to know."

She nodded and stood. "Thank you," she said, gathering her dignity like a cloak around her. "I'll go and freshen up." She went back to the rest room and waited until the door closed firmly behind her before she faced herself in the mirror.

Her reflection wasn't a reassuring sight. Somehow she'd managed to turn a rather bilious color of green. No doubt the altitude contributed to the sickly pallor.

She quickly used the facilities, washed her hands and face, and tried to rub some color—other than green—into her face before she had to return to the cabin.

There were times when Brad caught her off guard

with his acute observations of her. Now that she was going to be in his company for most of the next few days, she needed to watch her every word and expression. He didn't need to see beneath her professional facade any more than he already had.

After patting her face dry, combing her hair and reapplying her lipstick, Rachel returned to her seat. Brad was already seated next to her. As soon as she buckled herself in, he took her right hand firmly in his large left one and said, "Hang on, Rachel, I won't let anything happen to you."

She had no idea whether he was referring to her mysterious stalker or to the interminable flight but it really didn't matter.

He was too late. Something had happened to her over which Brad Phillips had no control. He held her vulnerable heart in his grasp, if he but knew.

Chapter Three

Rachel kept her eyes closed and gratefully clasped Brad's hand during the landing. She no longer cared if she saved face or not. She'd given herself away on this flight and there was no going back.

Once the plane taxied to a hangar and stopped, Brad said, "You can open your eyes now." When she opened them Brad was watching her with a revolting grin on his face. "It's all right, Rachel. We're safely down and I really need my hand to unbuckle my seat belt."

She was mortified. She jerked her hand away from his and fumbled to release herself from the seat. He rose and held out his hand to her.

"Ready?" he asked with what she felt was undue amusement dancing in his eyes.

"You think this is funny, don't you?" she asked, ignoring his hand while she slipped the strap of her purse over her shoulder and stood.

"You have to admit there aren't many times when I see you less than your competent, professional self. At least let me enjoy it for a few minutes."

She picked up her briefcase, walked past him and headed to the door that the pilot had opened. "Live it up," she muttered crossly and gave the pilot a dazzling smile to make certain he knew that she wasn't disgruntled because of him.

Halfway down the steps, Rachel spotted Carl leaning against a late-model Jeep that she now remembered he'd driven from home. She waved with a sense of relief disproportionate to the moment, she knew, but she didn't care.

She'd had a rough day. Brad's ridiculous insistence that he protect her had only added to her stress. At least Carl would be there to lend her emotional support if she needed to distance herself from Brad during this trip.

Carl was in his mid-fifties, with a thick head of blindingly white hair. He was gruff, tough and highly competent. He was also a teddy bear. She'd never forget his beaming face last year when he'd come to the office with photos of his first grandchild, a brand-new little girl. He'd insisted that Chrissie looked exactly like her mother—his daughter—when she was born. All Rachel saw was a red face, squinting eyes and fists clenched as though the infant was ready to take on the world.

Once her feet touched the solid tarmac she gave a huge sigh of relief and headed toward Carl without checking to see if Brad was behind her.

When she reached the Jeep, Carl straightened from his leaning position and gave her a quick hug. "It's great to see you, Carl," she said.

He pulled his head back and looked at her. "You look a little green around the gills, honey. What's the boss been doing to you?" he asked with concern.

Brad spoke from somewhere behind her. "Forcing her to fly, it appears. Can't imagine how she's managed to hide that particular fear from me all these years." The two men shook hands.

While everyone got into the Jeep, Carl said, "I'll admit I was surprised to hear that you were bringing Rachel. I wondered if you thought you couldn't face Mrs. Crossland without help."

Rachel was thankful to be sitting directly behind Brad. She grinned without fear of his spotting her amusement. She glanced to the front and caught Carl's eyes in the rearview mirror. He winked before returning his gaze to the road.

"Rachel needed to get out of town for a few days," Brad said casually. "We were discussing the matter when you called. I decided this would be a good way to deal with both situations at the same time."

Once again Carl's gaze met hers in the mirror. "What's been happening while I've been away?"

She gave her head a slight shake before saying, "Oh, I was just asking for some time off." She gave him a smile of reassurance, then blinked in surprise when Carl laughed uproariously as though thinking of some private joke.

"Well, that certainly explains Brad's panic," Carl said after a moment. "Rachel, don't you know the whole company would collapse without you to run interference with the boss for the rest of us?"

Brad turned his head toward Carl, giving Rachel a view of his distinctive profile. If possible, his strong jaw seemed more pronounced when he said, "*You* don't seem to have trouble dealing with me without Rachel's help." His drawl was more pronounced.

Ah, so Carl's remark had pushed one of Brad's buttons.

Carl continued to watch the road as they barreled down the highway. "Well, yeah, but that's because I can always retire when you decide to fire me."

Brad snorted. "That'll be the day. I can see you staying at home playing with that grandbaby of yours all day. You'd be chomping at the bit looking for a little excitement within a week."

Carl laughed again. "Maybe so. Never can tell until I've tried it, though." Then in a more serious voice, he asked, "You want to hear about Mrs. Crossland's complaints?"

Brad shook his head. "Not until we get settled in. Is there going to be room for us at the condo you rented?"

Carl nodded. "You bet. There's three bedrooms, three baths. The place is cantilevered down a rather steep hill overlooking the resort's golf course, so there's a master bedroom at the very top, living-dining area and kitchen on the middle level, and the other two bedrooms are on the lowest floor. Every bedroom has a great view. It won't take me long to move my things out of the top bedroom.''

"Nonsense. Stay where you are. We won't be here long enough for you to inconvenience yourself. I'm sure the other bedrooms will work out fine.''

Carl risked another glance at the rearview mirror and raised his brows slightly. Rachel smiled and gave a slight nod of reassurance. So, she thought, amused. Carl was looking out for her, was he? Frankly, Rachel didn't care where she slept. Despite the early hour—the sun was still up—she was more than ready to call it a day and to seek the sweet oblivion of sleep.

"Sounds like you found a great place to stay while you're here,'' Brad said, glancing at the passing rural landscape.

"It's the nicest thing about the job at the moment. Did you know that the condo overlooks Lake Lure? I've been told that a few movies have been filmed in the area.''

Rachel leaned forward. "Really? Which ones?''

"I can think of a couple—*Dirty Dancing* and *Last of the Mohicans*. I get the impression the locals are pleased to share that information with the tourists who visit in droves each summer.'' After a moment Carl continued. "Too bad I don't play golf. I would have been out on the course this week just to let off steam. It would have been great to picture Mrs. Crossland's face on each golf ball every time I swung.''

Brad relaxed against his seat and chuckled. "Why

Carl, I'm beginning to think that maybe you don't like our client's wife.''

''She's an interfering, annoying irritant that I could certainly do without. It's difficult to find skilled construction people out here in the hills. What I don't need is for Mrs. Crossland to run them off with her withering remarks and snobbish criticisms about the work being done.''

''Has that become a problem?'' Brad asked, straightening.

''The best carpenter I have—a local whose cabinetwork would make a grown man cry tears of appreciation—stomped off the job just before I called you today saying he wasn't going to work another minute if that woman insisted on coming to the site every day. There were others mumbling about following him. That's when I called you.''

''Okay. I'll deal with it. Does she know I'm here?''

''Nope. The less I say to the woman, the easier it is for me to control my temper. She has no idea how much forbearance I've shown since she arrived.''

The men lapsed into silence when Carl turned off the interstate highway and followed winding two-lane roads that reminded Rachel of an earlier era—a time when people relaxed after a day of work, unaware of the term *stress*. Maybe Brad had been right to bring her. She might decide to stay in North Carolina for a while when Brad returned to Texas.

She leaned back in her seat and closed her eyes, feeling herself relax for the first time in several hours.

The sound of Carl's voice woke her some time later

when she heard him say, "Hell, Brad, what have you been doing to her, working her to death?"

Rachel sat up and looked around. They were no longer moving. Instead, the Jeep was parked in a large lot surrounded by condominium units. The view of the surrounding area was spectacular. The distant hills and a brief view of the lake looked like a backdrop to a movie set. No wonder the film industry had decided to use the place.

Brad held out his hand and assisted her from the back seat.

"Wow," she said reverently. "Why haven't I ever heard about this place?"

Carl grinned. "It's the state's best-kept secret. Everyone who discovers it is loath to have others discover it and move here as well."

Brad stretched and asked, "Which unit is yours?"

Carl nodded his head to the building directly in front of them. "The first one in that building." He paused, leaning into the Jeep to look around. "Did you forget your bags on the plane?" he asked, only now aware that all they carried were briefcases.

"Nope," Brad said, striding toward the condo. "I figured we could pick up whatever we need somewhere around here."

Carl turned to Rachel. "Is he kidding?"

"Unfortunately, no."

"Wish he'd said something before we left Asheville. The closest town with a shopping mall is about twenty-five miles away."

She sighed. "I'm not sure I can make it. I really am exhausted."

"Not to hurt your feelings or anything, but you do look a little weary." He watched Brad start up the walkway. "We better let him in before he starts yelling for the key. Come on, maybe I have something you can wear to tide you over till morning."

If she weren't so tired, Rachel would have laughed at the idea of six-foot-four-inch, two-hundred-forty-pound Carl helping her out in the clothes department.

"I may take you up on that," she finally said, walking with him to the door. "A T-shirt would be welcome for me to use tonight."

She and Carl joined Brad at the front door. Carl opened it and the three of them walked inside. The first thing she saw were two sets of stairways, one leading downward, the other one going up.

Carl led the way upstairs to two rooms that were divided by a large stone fireplace. Each room had large sliding doors at the other end that led onto a railed balcony.

"Not too shabby, Carl," Brad said after a soft whistle. "I admire your taste."

"The only reason I took this place was that the house we're building is no more than ten minutes away. This was the most convenient rental available."

Rachel looked around with interest. The place was fully furnished, including kitchen supplies. The dark-red carpet looked regal. There was a television set as well as a VCR. All the comforts of home, she thought.

Carl turned and pointed upward. "I sleep up there. The view's terrific, as you can imagine."

Brad and Rachel dutifully turned toward the stairway that stretched to yet another floor. They realized that the bedroom on the top floor was the size of the combined rooms where they stood, except for a small landing at the top of the stairs.

"There's a smaller balcony up there, as well," Carl said.

Rachel went back down the steps to the lowest floor. There was a closed door on each side of the hallway. She opened one and peeked in. She saw a bedroom with the same view of the hills and lake. She turned and opened the other door, which revealed an identical bedroom.

She had no idea which room Brad might want, but decided not to worry about it. She walked into the one to the left and closed the door, leaning against it with a sense of relief.

She shook her head and pushed herself away from the door. With her purse still hanging from her shoulder, Rachel walked into the large bathroom, which had a shower separate from the Jacuzzi-type tub.

She placed her purse on the counter and emptied it. She had the toiletry bag that contained a toothbrush and paste she'd purchased at the airport before Brad hauled her away from the public area to where the company plane awaited.

Thank goodness she carried moisturizing cream, a small brush and comb and a few items of makeup in her purse. They would get her through the next few hours.

Her suit looked tired, she thought, staring into the mirror ruefully. It wouldn't have taken her more than a few minutes to gather a few things if Brad hadn't been in such a hurry.

He didn't have a problem. Once on the plane he'd mentioned the items of clothing he kept in his briefcase. He could be so infuriating at times. What could he be thinking to drag her to North Carolina? She had no reason to go to the site or sit in on meetings Brad might have with the clients.

Oh, well, none of that mattered now. She was here. She might as well make the best of it.

Rachel systematically removed and folded each item of apparel before she turned on the stinging spray in the shower. After she adjusted the temperature, she pulled the pins from her hair, and then stepped into the shower.

She couldn't remember enjoying anything quite this much, she thought, as she allowed the water to flow over her head and body. The rental management had provided bath and face soap, as well as small bottles of shampoo and conditioner.

She unwrapped the bath soap and rigorously scrubbed her body until it tingled, then shampooed her hair. When her legs felt as if they had turned into limp noodles, she reluctantly turned off the water and stepped onto the mat beside the shower stall.

A luxuriously large towel hung on a rack nearby. She quickly towel-dried her hair before patting herself dry. Only then did she spot the terry cloth robe suspended from a hook on the back of the door. She wondered if Carl had left it, but when she drew closer, she saw the resort logo above a chest pocket. Without hesitating she pulled it down and wrapped the thick, soft material around her, sliding her arms into the sleeves.

Rachel returned to the bedroom, closed the drapes and slid beneath the covers of the bed. She closed her eyes with a sigh and fell asleep.

Brad stood at the sliding door of the living room with his hands in his pockets, staring out at the view. The sun had disappeared behind a cliff west of the condo, causing a blue mist to settle over the golf course below.

He'd never learned how to play golf, which was just as well, he supposed. When would he have had time to indulge himself in the sport?

He heard a noise behind him and turned to see Carl behind the kitchen bar making coffee.

"Good idea," Brad said, strolling over to one of the tall stools arranged in front of the kitchen bar.

"Thought you could use a cup before I make my report," Carl replied.

"Sorry to have put you off about Mrs. Crossland. I've had a number of things on my mind, not the least of which is Rachel's decision to take a leave of absence from the office. She sprang that one on me this morning. I was still reeling when you called. I'm hoping that while we're here, we can look at alternatives that aren't quite so drastic.''

Carl kept his gaze focused on the ground coffee he was measuring into the holder before he turned to Brad. He folded his massive arms across an equally impressive chest and leaned against the counter.

"I know what a loss it would be for you if Rachel decides to leave. I hope you can work something out.''

"So do I. Now then, tell me about Mrs. Crossland,'' Brad said, focusing on the immediate problem.

"Have you ever met her?''

Brad rubbed his chin thoughtfully before replying. "I don't believe so. All my meetings were with Crossland.''

"If that's the case, it's going to be difficult for you to understand the dynamics going on here,'' Carl said with a weary headshake.

"So tell me.''

"Mrs. Crossland is a second wife, or that's my guess, anyway. I got the impression that her husband is considerably older than she is.''

"He's probably your age,'' Brad said. "How old is she?''

"Hard to tell. She dresses like one of the Dallas Cowboy cheerleaders during a game—short-midriff kind of tops that barely cover her rather impressive assets…tiny shorts that look like she might have had them painted on…high-heeled sandals inappropriate to be wearing around a construction site.''

"I'm beginning to get the picture," Brad muttered, feeling a headache coming on in more ways than one.

"She has long, thick, probably bleached blond hair that she wears carefully arranged to suggest she just crawled out of bed." Carl pulled down a couple of mugs from one of the cabinets and filled them with the freshly brewed coffee. He inhaled appreciatively before handing one of the cups to Brad.

"Hell, Carl, sounds like you've done everything but take her measurements. Does your wife know about this?"

"Damn right. I call Joyce every night with complaints and questions about what makes a woman like her tick. Never met anyone quite like her."

Brad grinned. "Then you're in luck. I keep stumbling over them at every social event I've attended since the business took off." He took a tentative sip of the fragrant liquid. "I'm curious. What does Joyce say about her?"

Carl chuckled. "That she sounds like a trophy wife. Got her a husband who can indulge her every whim...and obviously does. I swear she behaves like a spoiled brat, inspecting each and everything that has been done and never satisfied with anything." He took a long swallow of coffee before setting down the cup with a thud. "I tell you, I can't take much more of this. If you can't get her to stay away from the place, I'm going to join the cabinetmaker and find something to do elsewhere."

"It's that bad?" Brad asked quietly.

"It's worse," Carl stated baldly. "Joyce has had

to talk me out of packing my gear and getting out of here for the past week.''

"Tell Joyce she deserves a bonus."

"*She* deserves a bonus. For what!"

"Keeping a cool head while you're losing yours, for starters."

Carl picked up his cup and walked around the bar to sprawl onto one of the stools. He placed his elbows on the counter and held the cup in front of his mouth with both hands.

"I'll call her right now, okay?" Brad said. "You have her number?"

Silently Carl fished into his shirt pocket and pulled out a business card. It belonged to Thomas Crossland, listing his telephone numbers in Dallas. Brad flipped the card over and saw a hand-printed number in a feminine hand.

Without moving from his perch, Brad reached for the wall phone and punched in the numbers in front of him.

The phone was answered on the second ring. A low, sultry voice answered. "Hello?"

"Mrs. Crossland?"

"Yes."

"This is Brad Phillips, Mrs. Crossland. I understand that—"

He got no further because she immediately jumped in with "Thank God you've called. I've been going out of my mind over here, trying to get someone with an ounce of intelligence to listen to me. They are ruining my home…absolutely *ruining* it. Those workers refuse to listen to anything I say. I really had no choice but to demand that someone contact you.''

Brad glanced at his watch. ''Have you had dinner, Mrs. Crossland?''

A surprised silence vibrated across the lines. ''Well, actually I haven't, but I don't see what that has to do with this mess.''

Brad kept his eyes on Carl as he replied. ''I thought we could talk about the matter over dinner, if that's all right with you.'' He waited.

''What? You mean you're actually here in North Carolina? I thought you were calling from Dallas!''

''No, ma'am. I'm here.''

''Well.'' She paused as though searching for words. ''That might work out all right. Tommy isn't here, though. He's in Europe doing God knows what…no doubt continuing to make more money than we'll ever be able to spend. I keep telling him there's no reason for him to work so hard. He's in the prime of his life. He should relax and enjoy some of the fruits of his labor, don't you think?''

Or, Brad thought, *he's finally decided he'd prefer to keep an ocean between him and his blushing bride.* He glanced at his watch. ''If you'll give me directions to your hotel, I'll be by to get you in an hour.''

She gave a trill of excited laughter. ''Oh, well. If you insist. I'm not in a hotel, though. There wasn't one close enough for me to keep an eye on the construction site. So I've rented a house.'' She gave him directions, which he dutifully wrote down, hoping Carl knew where the named roads were located.

"I'll see you soon," he said, as she continued to talk about the problems she was dealing with after she'd given him the necessary directions. Before she could say anything more, he hung up.

"Whew. Can that woman talk!" he said, turning back to Carl. He handed him the scribbled directions. "Does this make any sense to you?"

Carl read them before nodding. "She's about ten miles farther along that last road we turned off of to come here. I don't think you'll have a problem finding the place."

Brad finished his coffee. "I'd much prefer to stay here this evening with you and…" His voice trailed off as he said, "…Rachel." He looked around. "Where'd she go, anyway?"

"I heard one of the downstairs showers running a while back. It's possible she's already gone to bed."

"Now? It's not even eight o'clock."

"From everything I've heard, she's had an eventful day. Maybe she's tired."

Brad thought about that for a moment. "Yeah. I'll catch you up on what's been happening with her when I get back from dinner." He stood. "Oh, is it all right if I borrow your Jeep?"

Carl tossed him the keys. "Be my guest, boss. Take all the time you need."

Brad headed downstairs, wondering about Carl's tone. It was obvious that he and Mrs. Crossland had clashed as soon as she arrived. He had never seen Carl this upset. Brad wasn't looking forward to tonight's meeting, but was determined to get the matter

settled. Carl was too good an employee to be lost over
something like this.

He'd developed some tough negotiating skills since
he'd been in business, Brad thought. How hard could
it be to convince this woman that everything was under control?

Brad paused at the bottom of the steps and looked
at the closed doors. He wondered which one Rachel
had chosen. If she'd gone to sleep, he didn't want to
disturb her. On the other hand, he didn't want to walk
right in with no warning. He did a quick "eeny,
meeny, miny, moe" before he knocked softly on one
of the doors.

There was no answer.

She was probably in the other one. He opened the
door and stepped into a shadowy bedroom. He started
across the floor to the bathroom without bothering to
turn on a light, wanting a shower before his business
meeting. He pushed the door open and immediately
knew he had the wrong room.

The faint scent of soap and shampoo hung in the
room. He didn't need to turn on a light to know that
this was the room Rachel had chosen.

Wouldn't you know?

He backed out silently and turned, facing the bed.
Now that his eyes had adjusted, he could see Rachel
with the covers pulled to her chin, her pale face surrounded by a cushion of her softly curling hair.

She looked so vulnerable lying there. He knew he
needed to go to the other bedroom. But he didn't.
Instead, he continued to look at her. She seemed

smaller, somehow. Not that she was all that big, but he always thought of her as having a commanding presence.

Now she looked like a young girl, sleeping the sleep of innocence.

He left the room and closed the door softly behind him. Who would have believed he would find any woman innocent? He'd always been convinced that even newborn girls came fully equipped with the skills to manipulate and scheme.

His mother had certainly given him a hard-earned education about what a woman could do to a man's heart, if he ever allowed one to get close enough. Yep, his mother could be called lots of things without a charge of libel or slander, but the one he kept reminding himself about was teacher. She'd taught him very early in life not to trust any female, no matter her age or her relationship to him.

The lesson had served him well.

But Rachel had proven to him that she was different from other women. She was honest and trustworthy. She had integrity. She'd convinced him that at least one woman in the world was nothing like the woman who had given birth to him.

Brad crossed the hall to the other bedroom, flipping on the light. It looked like the twin to the one Rachel occupied. He strode to the bathroom for a quick shower. The sooner he met with Mrs. Crossland, the sooner he could calm Carl down so this job could finish in the black.

Chapter Four

Brad found Mrs. Crossland's rental without incident. The house sat back from the road at the end of a winding driveway lined with large stately trees. He drove the length of the driveway and parked in front of a detached two-car garage.

A comfortable-looking veranda wrapped around the front of the house and both sides. The outside light shone brightly and displayed colorfully upholstered cushions and pads placed on a casual sofa and a few chairs.

Not a bad rental, he thought as he climbed the stairs to the front door. He pressed the doorbell and waited.

He saw her shadow through the elaborately etched glass in the solid oak door, but even with Carl's description, Brad was startled at the vision that opened the door.

Mrs. Crossland looked to be in her late twenties, possibly early thirties, and could easily have stepped from the centerfold of a men's magazine.

What Carl had neglected to mention was that Mrs. Crossland was strikingly beautiful. Brad figured she stood about five feet ten inches tall in her stocking feet. In the spiked heels she wore tonight, she was almost as tall as he.

She'd gathered up her brightly colored hair into some kind of topknot with loose curls falling around her ears and neck. He couldn't figure out how she'd done it, but her face was so skillfully made up that her skin looked as dewy as a young girl's. Her large, cerulean-blue eyes looked nothing like a young girl's, however. They practically shouted her sensuality and her willingness to get to know him in a much more intimate setting than a dinner meeting.

Her dress was made from some sort of shimmery material that Brad didn't recognize except to know it was expensive. The champagne color set off her deeply tanned body. The dress was amazingly conservative—considering what Carl had told him about the revealing clothes she wore to the site—with its high neckline and long sleeves, although the clinging material managed to call attention to her full breasts, small waist and flaring hips. Its straight skirt ended at her knees—revealing long, slender legs.

She extended her hand. "You must be Bradley Phillips," she said, her voice low and intimate. "Tommy never mentioned how young you are to be the owner of such a large company." Amusement echoed in her husky voice. "I can't tell you how much I appreciate your taking time out from your busy schedule to meet with me." She gestured toward the inside of the house. "Would you like to come in for an aperitif before dinner?"

Brad found it difficult to look away from her. Here was temptation to any man who had an ounce of red blood running through his veins.

Carl must be having a good laugh about now at Brad's expense.

He smiled politely. "I made reservations for us. I understand the eating establishments around here close earlier than we're used to in Dallas. Perhaps we should leave now."

She thrust her bottom lip out in a provocative moue, as though she'd been deprived of much more than a drink before dinner.

"Well, if you insist," she said, turning away to pick up a satin evening bag. She glanced seductively over her shoulder and added, "We'll have to plan for after-dinner drinks when we return."

He wasn't paying all that much attention to her words because his attention was on her bare shoulders, long bare spine and the slight curve of her derriere that was revealed before the backless dress mercifully hid the rest of her from view.

He took a deep breath. "Uh, yeah, okay," he said absently. Not that he had any intention of walking into that house with her either now or later. She gave a very distinctive message in her every look, not to mention her choice of clothes. If any man crossed that threshold he would find her wrapped around him like a sinuous snake intent on its next meal. Brad had a strong suspicion she already had him in her sights.

He escorted her to the Jeep and opened the passenger door. She delicately placed her hand in his as though she needed help. This close, he couldn't ignore the scent of her provocative perfume.

Good grief, he thought, this woman is lethal to a man's peace of mind. He could certainly understand why Tom Crossland might consider her a trophy.

Brad had a moment of sympathy for Tom. If Mrs. Crossland came on to *him* like this, how did she behave around other men? The sexual energy radiating from her made him a little light-headed.

He reminded himself that Mrs. Crossland had already caused him a great deal of trouble and possibly a delay in completing the project. By the time he slid into the driver's seat, his mind had cleared somewhat. He focused on the reason for this meeting and how necessary it was for him to appease her without running up cost overruns that her husband might refuse to pay.

He started the Jeep and turned it around in the driveway. She placed her hand with its taupe-colored nails lightly against his coat sleeve. "I'm so pleased to be able to meet you at long last. Tommy is always singing your praises. I understand that you've built more than one of his projects. Is that right?"

"Yes." He drove back to the two-lane highway and turned toward the private club that tenants of the condos were invited to use.

"He told me that he really had to talk long and hard to convince you to help us with our summer home here in the Carolinas."

"All my work is located in and around Texas."

Her warm chuckle caressed his senses. "Then we are indeed lucky to have convinced you to make an exception in our case."

He kept his mouth shut on several responses he could make. He reminded himself that Tom Crossland was a good client who had recommended him to several potential clients. There was no reason to alienate him by offending his wife.

When they pulled into the driveway of the restaurant she said, "Oh, how marvelous. I've always wanted to come here but haven't really had the time. You must have read my mind."

If her body language, tone of voice and choice of apparel hadn't signaled her availability so blatantly, he might have thought he *could* read her mind. From the glances she kept casting his way, he would guess that what she had in mind for after dinner was probably against the law in more than one state.

Now that it was too late, he wished he'd waited until tomorrow to meet with Mrs. Crossland. Rachel's presence was needed to emphasize the business nature of the meeting.

Brad escorted Mrs. Crossland into a quiet, dimly lit dining room. The room appeared to be full of patrons. As soon as he gave the maître d' his name, they were led to a table for two that no doubt had a lovely view of the surrounding area. Unfortunately, it was too dark at this hour to appreciate the gesture of seating them there. He smiled and gave the man a nod of approval.

Once seated, Brad studied the menu, suddenly feeling exhausted. He envied Rachel peacefully sleeping at the condo. He should have followed her example.

He glanced toward his guest and asked, "Have you decided what you would like, Mrs. Crossland?"

She smiled at him, a slow, intimate smile that would have been more appropriate for a bedroom setting. "Please. No one calls me Mrs. Crossland. That title belongs to Tommy's mother. My name is Katherine, but I insist that you call me Kat. I hope that since Tommy refers to you as Brad, that you might allow me the same privilege."

Her voice had become a soft purr. His body reacted to her but his mind and emotions were coolly observing the interplay. Was this the way she got her way? By attempted—sometimes successful—seduction?

Once again he had his parents to thank for the early—and painful—lessons he'd learned about women.

"I'd be more comfortable calling you Katherine," he replied smoothly.

She wrinkled her nose and gave a slight shrug. "Well, I certainly want you to be comfortable—" she gave the word a particularly seductive emphasis "—by all means."

He wondered if she was putting him on to see what kind of response she might get. If so, good old Tommy would hear about any unprofessional conduct

on his part before the night ended. Katherine must
enjoy taunting any male with whom she came into
contact. She was certainly enjoying the covert glances
from the men at other tables.

His mind soon disciplined his unruly body. As he
had told Carl, he'd been exposed to women like Katherine Crossland before, but he had to tread lightly not
to lose Tom as a client. It was obvious that Katherine
didn't care about possible fallout as a result of her
behavior.

Once he faced that, her looks and behavior no
longer affected him.

After several minutes of dithering on her part over
the list of entrées, Brad managed to get her to select
one.

The hovering waiter appeared to receive their orders. Once the waiter left, Brad said, "Why don't you
tell me what seems to be the problem with the construction of your home?"

Her husky laugh caused a few of the nearest oc-
cupants to glance their way. "The biggest problem is
that Tommy and I tend to disagree on what a summer
home should be. He wanted something rustic and in-
formal in contrast to our home in Dallas. Of course I
told him that regardless of where we live, we have
certain standards to maintain. I thought he was clear
on that, but now that I see the house being built, I
realized I wanted some changes made to his rather
quaint ideas. I see no reason why your men can't
honor my suggestions."

Brad tried to think of something diplomatic to say.

His headache had continued to worsen as this nightmare meeting dragged on. "Mrs. Crossland—" She held up her hand in a stop motion and he amended himself. "Katherine, according to the man in charge of this project, your suggestions would cost several thousand dollars more than Tom agreed to pay. We can't make those changes without his written approval."

"Not even when his wife gives her permission?"

"Not even then. However, if you'll have Tom contact me, we can discuss the changes you want to make and can go from there."

She shook her head wearily. "This is all too absurd. It isn't as though we don't have the money to pay for any changes I might make to the original plans."

He nodded. "Of course you do. If you had suggested these changes to the architect when he drew up the plans, we would have no problem implementing them."

She studied him for several moments before she said, "You aren't going to do this for me, are you? You're going to stick to all your petty rules and not listen to a thing I want."

"How about if we meet at the site tomorrow and see what we can do without running up the tab too much. Would you be willing to do that?"

The waiter brought their meals, and Brad stared at his food, wishing he'd settled for a sandwich. His headache made the rich food on his plate distasteful.

Katherine waited until their after-dinner coffee had

arrived before she answered his earlier question. "Thank you for at least listening to me. Sometimes I feel invisible. Tom does what he wants without considering what I'd like." She smiled at him. "Are you married, Brad?" she asked.

Now there was a loaded question in her present frame of mind. He searched his brain for a suitable answer and was getting a little desperate when he thought of Rachel, who had traveled to North Carolina for business purposes, after all. He definitely needed her as a buffer on this particular job.

"Not exactly," he replied, hoping she would read all kinds of hidden meaning in the words. Maybe she would let it go at that.

No such luck.

"What does that mean?" she asked, a hint of sharpness in her voice.

Now what? He didn't want to lie. That wasn't the way he worked. He'd seen enough scams and lies in his life to consider the truth a sacred trust.

So, what was the truth about his relationship with Rachel that might help him in this situation?

"There's someone very special to me. I couldn't do without her." True enough, he thought.

"I see," she responded thoughtfully. "I'd love to meet her sometime."

"That's easy enough to do. I'll bring her with me tomorrow and introduce you."

"Oh," she said faintly. "She travels with you?"

"Occasionally," he said, which was true. He saw

no reason to add that this was the first time he'd flown with her.

The waiter appeared and discreetly placed the bill near Brad's elbow. Brad immediately placed a credit card in the folder, anxious for this meeting to be over.

Katherine remained silent on the way back to her house. When they arrived he helped her out of the Jeep and escorted her to the front door. She unlocked it and turned to him.

"You aren't going to come in for an after-dinner drink, are you?" she asked, sounding resigned.

"No."

"I hope your friend isn't upset about our having dinner tonight." Her tone conveyed the opposite hope.

Brad smiled. "She knew this was a business meeting. I would have brought her with me but she decided to get some rest, instead."

Katherine stared at him in silence as though memorizing his face. "She's a very lucky woman," she finally said, softly, then turned and went inside, shutting the door behind her.

That takes care of that, he thought, feeling uncomfortable. He had told the strict truth but implied so many things that weren't true. Maybe it was a case of wishful thinking on his part.

Brad returned to the condo more tired than he could ever remember being. The day hadn't gotten off to a good start and had gone downhill from there.

He strode across the parking lot to the front door of the condo. As soon as he let himself in, he realized that Carl had left a light on upstairs for him. He climbed the steps to the living/dining area and paused, staring into the compact kitchen in surprise.

Rachel stood at the stove, making something. She looked smaller than usual. Whether it was because he'd just spent the past few hours with an Amazon-sized woman, or whether it was because Rachel wore an oversized robe and was barefooted, he didn't know.

Her long hair tumbled around her shoulders and down her back. She must have heard him come in, because she glanced casually around and said, "You hungry?"

He shook his head.

"Well, I'm starved. I woke up with my stomach growling, so I found the makings of an omelet. I also discovered some leftover coffee. It was cold, so I made a new pot. Want some?"

All he'd wanted to do when he walked into the condo was to go to bed. However, the freshly brewed coffee smelled too good to ignore.

"Yeah. Although I don't think all the caffeine in the world is going to keep me awake for long."

She looked him up and down, no doubt noticing that he'd already altered his appearance somewhat. He'd unbuttoned the top two buttons of his shirt and taken off his tie as soon as he'd dropped Katherine Crossland at her house. He'd walked inside with his suit jacket tossed over one shoulder. He dropped it on the back of one of the chairs and sat at the bar, rolling up his shirtsleeves.

Rachel filled two cups and set them on the bar before turning back to the stove. ''So how did the meeting go? Were you able to address her concerns?'' she asked, slipping her steaming omelet onto a plate.

He watched as she came around the bar and sat next to him. He swiped his hand over his face, wondering how to answer. The question was straightforward enough; the answer much more complicated.

He decided he was too tired to be diplomatic. ''I listened to her complaints, explained about the contract her husband signed, then agreed to meet her at the site tomorrow,'' he related tersely. ''The only problem I had was convincing the lady I was not interested in lingering at her place after dinner.''

Rachel had a bite of food on her fork halfway to her mouth when he spoke. She froze and stared at him. ''Are you saying she came on to you?''

Her incredulity amused him. ''Well, I could explain that most women have that kind of reaction when they're out to dinner with me—'' Her huff of indignation was the response he'd hoped for. He relaxed and picked up his cup before adding, ''However, the truth is I don't think she cared who I was as long as I bought into her seductive siren act.''

''Oh, my,'' Rachel said, ducking her head. She quickly took the bite of food waiting on her fork.

''Don't bother trying to hide your amusement. I guess I would find the whole thing amusing, too, if her complaints hadn't pulled me away from more productive work in Texas.''

''What is her biggest concern?''

"About the project? I never heard the particulars. Her primary agenda appeared to revolve around whether or not she had convinced me that she was hot to jump my bones."

"Were you?"

Her eyes twinkled with amusement and he found himself gazing at her with all the yearning that he hadn't felt while he was with Katherine Crossland.

He gave his head a quick shake. Man, he was more tired than he thought. He must have jogged something loose in his brain earlier when he used Rachel to convince Katherine he had certain commitments that he wouldn't ignore for her sake.

"Go ahead and laugh," he said. "Tomorrow is your turn."

"For what?"

"Mrs. Crossland somehow got the impression that you and I are involved. I did nothing to discourage her from gaining that impression. I told her I'd bring you with me to the site tomorrow so she could meet you. She's going to be there to point out the changes she wants made and I'll tell her whether or not I can do them without getting her husband's written approval."

She ignored most of his explanation and zeroed in on the part he'd wanted to downplay. "You don't know how she got that impression, huh?" Rachel repeated with raised brows.

"Okay, so I'm hiding behind you. So sue me."

She grinned. "You really must have been desperate. Remind me to buy something provocative to wear tomorrow.''

He didn't need to see her in something provocative. The last thing he needed right now was to fantasize about his assistant. The situation was precarious enough. This was the first time they had shared the same living space; the first time he'd seen her in a robe, barefoot, with her hair loose.

He repeated his thought out loud. ''I don't think I've ever seen you with your hair loose like that.''

She blinked at him in surprise. ''That's because I always have it pinned up while I'm working.''

He watched as his hand reached out as though independent of him. ''You have beautiful hair,'' he murmured, lightly running his hand down the back of her head before slipping his fingers around a long curl.

She looked at him suspiciously. ''Exactly how much did you have to drink tonight, Brad?''

He jerked his hand away. ''Sorry. Don't know what I was thinking. I'm half-asleep as I sit here.'' He sighed, a wave of fatigue sweeping over him. ''I apologize.'' He raised his cup and drained it. ''I'm going to hit the sack.'' He looked at her, wrapped up in a robe several times too large for her, looking like an adorable child wearing adult clothing. ''We'll run to town early in the morning and get something to wear. We could have stopped before we left Asheville but I totally forgot to say anything to Carl. It seems to be my night to apologize to you.''

Rachel gracefully slipped off the stool and faced

him. "Brad? Are you all right?" The concern in her voice touched something deep within him that he had never known existed.

He frowned, uncomfortable with the fleeting sense of vulnerability that had momentarily gripped him. "Of course I am. And no, I haven't been drinking. I'm just tired, that's all. We'll talk in the morning." He headed to the steps leading down to the bedrooms.

"Brad?"

He reluctantly turned around. "Yeah?"

"Can we go back home tomorrow?"

He looked down the stairwell as though to find the answer woven into the fabric of the rug. "I'd like to, Rachel. It will depend on how the meeting goes. If not tomorrow, we'll leave no later than Friday. I can either resolve the matter or contact Tom to find out what he wants me to do."

"Do you think Carl knew what would happen when you met with her?"

He shook his head wearily. "I don't have a clue." He continued down the stairs, adding, "I'll see you in the morning."

Brad felt as if he had to escape before he said or did something totally out of line where Rachel was concerned. What was wrong with him? A very beautiful woman had used her considerable skills and assets in an effort to seduce him and he'd been able to walk away without a backward glance. Yet the sight of Rachel with no makeup, wearing a too-big robe and barefoot had caused such a surge of lust in him that he was still shaking from the necessity of hiding his response from her.

He walked into his room and closed the door. All he needed was a good night's sleep. He stripped off his clothes, disgusted that he was still half-aroused from his unexpected encounter with Rachel.

The very last thing he needed to further complicate his life was to become fixated on a woman. To fixate on Rachel spelled absolute disaster.

Rachel finished her omelet and had another cup of coffee before she returned to the kitchen to clean up. When she came out of the kitchen she caught a glimpse of something white draped across one of the dining-room chairs. She walked over and discovered that Carl had left her one of his T-shirts to sleep in.

With a smile she turned out the lights, took the shirt and returned to her room. After she put on Carl's thoughtful gift, she almost laughed out loud at the sight in the mirror. The shirt that fitted him so well hung to her knees and fell off one shoulder. But she would be more comfortable sleeping in the shirt than in the bulky robe.

Rachel stretched out and closed her eyes. Instead of falling asleep she reviewed what Brad had told her about his evening.

He'd been irritated that Mrs. Crossland had stepped over the line between business and personal matters. Of course he would be. Not only was she the wife of one of his clients, she no doubt reminded him of what he worked diligently to ignore—that he was human, just like the rest of us. Too bad he wouldn't admit that being tempted wasn't the same thing as yielding to temptation.

She'd not seen him in such a strange mood before. He must have panicked to have implied that he was involved with her. Perhaps that was the only thing he could think of to help Mrs. Crossland save face. No doubt she could accept that he was committed to another woman, but would be hurt and angered if he'd rebuffed her because he wasn't interested.

What had startled Rachel was his stroking her hair. He had never touched her so intimately. She'd felt at her most vulnerable with him tonight *before* he'd touched her because she'd been very aware that she wore nothing beneath the robe.

Earlier, when she'd gone upstairs to find something to eat, she had thought that both men were already in bed. Hearing Brad's key in the door caught her by surprise. It was too late to run downstairs and throw on her clothes…or do something with her hair…so she had dealt with the situation as calmly as possible.

The fact that he had been disturbed about his evening had helped her to relax. His mind was on other things than how she was dressed. His mentioning her appearance abruptly destroyed not only her theory but her peace of mind.

Tomorrow will be better, she thought. Once she had some fresh clothes to wear, she'd feel more relaxed about their situation. Staying in the same condo had thrown them into a new dynamic for which neither of them was prepared.

With any luck, Brad would work his usual magic tomorrow and calm everyone so that work on the house could move toward completion on schedule. Either way they would return to Dallas no later than Friday, which meant she only needed to get through tomorrow and tomorrow night. After that they would resume their familiar roles.

The only real problem she had at the moment was what to do about the intruder in her home and life. The time she'd spent out of her normal routine had helped her to gain some perspective, but nothing had removed the fear that the thought of the stalker stirred in her.

Instead of leaving town, perhaps she could find another, more secure place to live. With the generous salary Brad paid her, she could afford to live wherever she wished. Perhaps that was the answer...find a new place to live and get on with her life.

She drifted to sleep, feeling that her life would soon be back on track.

The next morning Rachel woke at her usual time, but since she was on eastern daylight time, she felt she was an hour late getting her day started. After a quick shower, she dressed, arranged her hair and put on whatever makeup she'd found in her purse.

She heard Carl and Brad talking as soon as she reached the first landing. The beckoning aroma of freshly made coffee moved her quickly up the remaining steps. As soon as she turned toward the kitchen the men spotted her, greeting her with gruff, early-morning voices.

She wasn't used to seeing men waking up over early-morning coffee, each sporting tousled hair and unshaven cheeks. It seemed a little too intimate to her, but there was little she could do about it.

Rachel responded to their greetings with a nod and brief smile before she headed for the coffeepot. Without turning to look at them she said, ''When are we going to the site?''

Brad answered. ''First things first. We have to wait until the stores open. Then we can go to the shopping mall Carl mentioned. I suggest we find something casual to wear, since we'll be at the construction site most of the day. Does that sound okay to you?''

She turned and faced him, leaning against the counter. He didn't look as though he'd slept very well, which was unfortunate for all of them. She'd dealt with him before when he was sleep-deprived and had managed to survive his surliness. She'd muddle through today, as well.

''Sounds more than okay. This unexpected trip has taught me always to keep a bag at the office in the future, just in case.'' She drank some of her coffee before adding, ''Especially with such an unpredictable boss.''

Brad refused to acknowledge her remark, but Carl chuckled. Brad sat with his head down, looking at his coffee. She didn't know why, but she had an impish desire to force him out of his bad mood. He needed to lighten up.

Straightening, she placed her cup on the counter with theirs and leaned toward them, her weight on her forearms. "It's tough being so irresistible, isn't it, boss man?"

Carl gave her a sharp look before turning his gaze to Brad. "Have I missed something?"

Brad shook his head. "Not really. I was a little irritated when I got in last night and unloaded on Rachel." He gave her a narrow-eyed stare. "I'd hoped she would forget some of that."

"Not a chance," she replied with a lilt. She looked at Carl and winked. "It seems that Mrs. Crossland had other activities in mind for the two of them in addition to discussing the problems she'd found with her home." She batted her eyelashes at Brad.

"I'm not amused," he replied coldly when Carl began to laugh.

"Aw, come on, boss," Carl said. "You've got to see the humor in all of this. The woman's been giving everyone on the job ulcers. It's only fair that you start a crop of your own."

Brad stood, draining his coffee mug. "Let's get out of here. I've had about all of the comedy routine I can stomach this early in the day."

"Sounds good," Carl replied. "I need to go to the site and get things moving. Since it's on your way to town, you can drop me off. I'll give you directions. You won't have trouble finding the mall."

"When are we supposed to meet Mrs. Crossland?" Rachel asked. There was no reason to continue to tease a tiger with a thorn in his paw.

"I don't think we set a time." Brad looked at Carl. "When does she generally show up?"

"Not before noon. At least we have the mornings to work without interruption."

After the men had shaved and prepared for the day, the three of them piled into Carl's Jeep with Rachel taking the back seat. She remained silent.

When they reached the site, Carl and Brad got out and Brad looked around the area. "You've done a hell of job getting this much done, with or without distractions."

"Thanks. Keep Mrs. Crossland away from here and I'll forego any bonus I might receive this year."

The first smile of the day appeared on Brad's face. "I don't think you need to sacrifice that much, but I'll see what I can do."

He turned and offered his hand to Rachel. When she had moved successfully to the front passenger seat, he listened to Carl's directions and slid into the driver's seat beside her.

They headed toward the mall Carl had recommended, neither of them speaking. She'd been alone with Brad countless times over the years but there was something different about today. He radiated a tension that she didn't understand. He wasn't worried about handling Mrs. Crossland, was he? She'd seen him worry about different business problems before, but she hadn't witnessed such quiet intensity.

What else could be going on with him? Asking him was pointless. He told her what he wanted her to know, so there was no use in wasting her breath.

The shopping mall loomed alongside the highway as they entered town. "Easy enough to find," she commented.

He made some unintelligible remark that sounded suspiciously like a caveman's grunt.

Once parked, Brad led the way to a large department store that was part of a national chain.

"Why don't we get something here?" he asked brusquely. "Keep your receipts for reimbursement."

"No," she replied. "Whatever I get will be added to my wardrobe and has nothing to do with the company."

"I'm the one who told you not to pack, that you could get what you need here."

"So you did and that's what I intend to do," she said firmly.

He glanced at her as they walked inside the store. "Has anyone ever mentioned that you can be stubborn?"

"Why no, I don't believe anyone has." She glanced at her watch. "When and where do you want to meet?"

"Say in an hour here by the front door. Will that give you enough time?"

"Certainly," she replied with dignity and marched to the escalator, which she rode to the second floor, where women's wear could be found, according to the store directory.

She quickly thumbed through circular racks, wondering what to get. He'd said casual. She never dressed casually. Well, almost never. She had a closet full of suits, blouses and practical shoes, all in muted colors.

As soon as she saw the full skirt, she knew exactly what she would get. She found a blouse, tossed in a summer suit that had been marked down to a great price, and went to the dressing rooms to change.

Pleased with her purchases, she wore the skirt and blouse and put her travel-worn suit—which she didn't intend to wear for a long while after this trip—into the bag with the new one. Then she headed to the shoe department.

Once there, she threw caution to the wind and bought a pair of sandals. No heel and nothing but a few straps. She loved them, and they looked great with her new outfit.

She could hardly wait to see Brad's reaction when he saw her.

Promptly on the hour, Rachel strolled down the aisle that led to the front doors. She'd taken time to get a few toiletries as well as a sleepshirt that said, Morning Doesn't Start Until I Say So.

Brad was already there, holding a bag with the store's logo. He had on a pair of khaki pants and a navy-blue short-sleeved pullover shirt. She fought her reaction. It would not do for Brad's administrative assistant to start drooling because he'd gone back to his early, working-construction look. Without the concealing jacket, his muscled arms and broad chest stood out in bold relief. Plus his pants fit snugly across his butt. She sighed. She could look, she reminded herself. She couldn't touch.

"Ready to go?" she asked quietly behind him. He'd been looking out the glass door and turned abruptly at the sound of her voice. His reaction was everything she'd hoped it would be. His eyes widened before narrowing and his face went carefully blank. He clenched his jaw, no doubt in order not to comment on her choice of apparel, because all he said was, "Yes. Let's go."

The walk to the Jeep was an adventure for Rachel. The breeze had picked up while they were inside and she had to fight the wide skirt to keep it from flying over her head.

The skirt was made from material painted with swirls of jewel tones—ruby red, emerald green, golden topaz and sapphire blue. She'd chosen to match the green in the skirt when she picked out her sleeveless blouse.

Her business hairdo hadn't looked right with her casual look, so she had brushed out her hair and secured it with several decorative combs she'd found in the store. As a final touch, she'd also bought a bright red lipstick and eye shadow that emphasized the green in her eyes.

Rachel felt practically barefoot in the sandals. In fact, she felt like a new woman. She was beginning to think that she was entirely too conservative in her dress and manner. This could be the first step in breaking out of her staid existence.

Today she felt like a gypsy.

Once again silence reigned on the drive back to the site. Brad appeared preoccupied. She took in the scenery, admiring the lush foliage and humming softly beneath her breath.

As soon as she stepped out of the Jeep after they arrived on site, Carl gave a wolf whistle that echoed around the area. Heads turned as he strode to greet them.

"Wow, Rachel. You look great in that outfit. You should wear bright colors more often. Don't you think so, Brad?"

He gave her a brief glance. "I guess. Have you heard from Mrs. Crossland?"

The two men started toward the building under construction.

Now what? she wondered. Her part wouldn't begin until Mrs. Crossland showed up. With time on her hands Rachel decided to explore the house. She'd grown used to being around construction sites during the years she'd worked at Phillips Construction Company. Her shoes weren't the most practical, but they were safer than the office pumps she generally wore.

Rachel picked her way across the yard, careful to avoid discarded debris that hadn't made it to the disposal bin. She paused at the top step of the porch and turned. The view made her throat close with sudden emotion. What a beautiful sight awaited anyone who chose to sit there and look out over the valley spread before her, the rolling hills serving as a backdrop. She swallowed and for a fleeting moment wondered what it would be like to live somewhere like this instead of in a busy city.

Brad spoke behind her, causing her to jump in surprise. "You know, all you need with that outfit is a rose between your teeth."

She turned and looked at him. "Great idea. I'll see what I can do to find one." She started toward the doorway that stood open.

Brad took her elbow, causing her to stop walking, and said, "I don't want you going anywhere without me while we're here."

He looked and sounded serious. Something must have happened that she'd missed. "What's wrong?"

His jaw clenched a couple of times before he said, "If you dressed to call attention to yourself today, you did a bang-up job. There's not a worker here who's been able to keep his mind on his work since you arrived. I don't want to have to fire someone for getting too familiar with you." He stared at her, his height pronounced because of her flat-heeled shoes. "You barely look eighteen in that outfit. Nobody would believe that you're a respected business-woman."

She could think of several scathing comments to make in reply, such as that he was the one who had mentioned the word *casual* for the clothes they were to buy, and that he was the one who had insisted that she make this trip without giving her a chance to bring appropriate attire.

She thought them but she didn't say them, which was why she'd remained with him all these years.

"I apologize if my choice of clothes causes you problems. I have other clothes in the Jeep. Where would you like me to change?"

He stepped away from her as though only now aware that he still held her arm. He faced the view from the front door rather than look at her. He stood there and she waited. When he turned back to her, his eyes were dark with an emotion she didn't recognize.

"There's no reason for you to change clothes. Look, I've been in a lousy mood, but there's no excuse for my taking it out on you and I'm sorry. You threw me a curve wearing that outfit today, that's all. I wasn't prepared for it…which isn't your problem." He glanced around at the men busy with various projects and lowered his voice. "However, I meant what I said about the men. We don't want any trouble here. They might think you're Carl's daughter and treat you with respect. We can only hope."

"I was hoping to look through the house. Do you have time to go with me?"

He smiled, but she knew his heart wasn't in it. "Sure. I need to familiarize myself with it before Mrs. Crossland arrives, anyway."

The sound of a power drill broke the tension between them. Without a word Rachel turned back to the house. After stepping over the unfinished threshold and into the hallway, she paused to remove her sunglasses. A curving stairway greeted her as it followed the rounded wall to the second floor.

She could already picture the Austrian crystal chandelier that would hang in the center of the foyer. She couldn't help but wonder how many months out of the year the Crosslands would make use of their second home.

Workers nodded as she wandered through the downstairs rooms, Brad following somewhere behind her. She'd been unnerved by their exchange. He was upset with her even though he denied it. But why? Because she'd teased him about Mrs. Crossland? He enjoyed a joke as well as anyone, even when it was on him...*especially* when it was on him. She wondered what invisible line she'd accidentally crossed.

After checking out the large kitchen, she took the back stairs to the second floor. When she reached the top, Rachel looked around to get her bearings and discovered that she stood in a broad hallway. One direction would take her to the front stairs, so she turned the other way. At the end of the hallway was a wide opening that would eventually be closed in with double doors. She stepped over the threshold and saw the layout for the master bedroom.

Now this was living, she decided.

A large skylight was over what she imagined would be the bed area. She walked over toward that wall and turned, enamored once again with the view. The wall opposite would be mostly glass. From there she could see the ground slope downward to a creek in the distance.

Brad hadn't followed her upstairs. Maybe he felt she was safe enough with him in the house. She had never seen him in such a strange mood and wasn't certain how to deal with it.

She concentrated on exploring the rest of the master suite, wishing the day were over so their return trip would be closer.

Rachel wandered into an alcove off the master bedroom and realized that there would be his-and-her dressing rooms with connecting walk-in closets.

The bathroom was the best feature yet, she thought, chuckling. There was room enough for a half-dozen people in the mammoth tub. The glass-enclosed shower was equally large. She could imagine the plush carpeting that would cover the floor. Unbelievable.

This house belonged to a couple with no children, which she found sad. The place begged for a family, a large one at that.

When Rachel returned to the main part of the master suite she was startled to see a woman standing in the middle of the room. This must be the famous—or infamous—Mrs. Crossland.

Brad had forgotten to mention last night that the woman was stunningly beautiful, or would be if it weren't for the disgruntled look on her face.

Rachel smiled at her but was greeted by a look of suspicion.

"You must wonder who I am, exploring your home like this," she said pleasantly.

"You know who I am?" Katherine asked, continuing to frown.

Rachel nodded. "I presume you're Mrs. Crossland, aren't you?"

"Oh! Then you must be Carl's daughter," Katherine replied, sounding relieved. "I was looking for Brad and thought he might be up here," she added. She turned and strolled toward the hallway door only to turn rather abruptly when Rachel chuckled and said, "Uh, no. I'm not kin to Carl at all. However, I—"

Brad's smooth baritone interrupted her. "Actually, she's with me," he said with a lazy drawl, appearing in the doorway. Rachel had never been so glad to see anyone as she was to see him standing there.

Katherine slowly turned to face him. "This must be the woman you mentioned to me last night. You didn't bother to tell me she's a mere child."

Rachel knew better than to respond to her remark. Instead, she looked at Brad and smiled. *The ball's in your court, boss man. You deal with it.*

His laugh sounded so sexy it startled her. "Oh, Rachel isn't as young as she appears—" He walked over to Rachel and dropped his arm around her shoulders. Looking down at her with a heated glance, he added, "Are you, honey?"

Rachel had an almost irresistible urge to leap away from the warmth of his body and his penetrating gaze. He must have felt her tense in preparation for such a move, because he calmly pulled her against his side, nestling her there as though the position was a natural one.

Rachel knew he wanted Katherine to believe they were close but she hadn't expected him to be quite so cozy with her. She heard a sound at the door and saw Carl standing there, taking in the scene with amusement.

He spoke to Brad, "There, I told you she hadn't gone far, didn't I?" before adding to Katherine, "He hates to let Rachel out of his sight, you know. That's why he insisted she come with him yesterday."

As soon as she saw the twinkle in Carl's eyes, Rachel realized that he'd decided to help with their role-playing. He seemed to be enjoying it. In that case, she might as well enjoy it, too. She relaxed against Brad's side and offered her most benign smile to Katherine, who did not look happy. In fact, she looked as if she might start spitting toads at any moment.

Brad said, "Thank you for meeting us here, Katherine. Why don't you show me the areas that are causing you concern?"

Rachel straightened slowly as though reluctant to lose contact with Brad. "I'll wait for you near the Jeep and let you get on with your work," she said.

Thinking that she'd played her part satisfactorily, Rachel took a step toward the door, only to be caught by the wrist and gently turned back to face him.

"I'll be there as soon as I can," he said in a husky voice, which Rachel thought was overdoing it just a mite, but it was nothing compared to his next move. He placed a gentle kiss on her mouth and rested his other hand on her neck, effectively holding her head in place.

Rachel knew the kiss meant nothing. What was a kiss, anyway? A casual show of affection, that's all. Had Rachel been in a calmer state of mind she could have accepted it as such. Except his lips lingered a little longer than was strictly necessary and she forgot that he didn't mean it.

As though freed from the frantic signals from her brain telling her to get out of there and fast, Rachel went up on her toes and returned the kiss, her arms sliding oh-so-naturally around his neck. At long last she'd been given the opportunity to compare the reality of being in his arms to fantasies she'd had over the years.

She savored the moment.

Carl cleared his throat in an obvious attempt to disguise a chuckle, which snapped Rachel out of her fog of indulgence and caused her to stare at Brad, immediately horrified by what she had just done.

His eyes had darkened until they were almost black; their message unmistakable. He clenched his jaw. In a voice too low for the others to hear, he murmured, "I won't keep you waiting long," as his hand shifted to the nape of her neck once more where he massaged the tensed muscles and nerves clustered there. "We have several things we need to discuss once we're alone."

Chapter Five

Rachel hung on to the temporary railing as she went down the winding staircase, not trusting her knees to support her. What had happened back there? Something alarming, something wondrous, something that changed a long-term business relationship into who knew what.

She paused once she reached the porch and took several deep and, she hoped, calming breaths before she negotiated the steps to the ground. She focused on reaching the Jeep without mishap, determined that any worker who might see her would think that nothing unusual had happened to her—although her personal universe had spun on its axis in the past few minutes and now hung upside down.

Brad Phillips had kissed her. He had behaved totally out of character. She hadn't been prepared for the kiss or for her strong reaction to it. She didn't know if she'd be able to face him after grabbing him like a love-starved woman.

Rachel reached the Jeep and sank into the front seat, thankful Brad had parked beneath a shade tree where it was cool, despite the midday heat. She closed her eyes, and fervently prayed to disappear before she had to face him again.

What caused her to tremble was remembering the heated look in Brad's eyes when she had finally pulled away from him.

Somehow, some way, she knew she had to get a grip on her emotions before he and Carl showed up at the Jeep.

She opened her eyes and consciously squared her shoulders. Face the dilemma, she thought. Treat the matter as a problem to be solved.

First of all, she owed Brad an apology. She ran a few through her head. "I'm sorry to have grabbed and kissed you," didn't work. Besides, it wasn't true. Embarrassed because she'd grabbed him…humiliated because she'd given away her secret feelings for him…those were all true. But sorry? Uh-uh. She'd wondered for too many years what kissing Brad would be like.

Well, she had certainly found out…in front of a client and an employee of the company. "I'm sorry for taking advantage of the situation?" That was closer to the truth. Brad had kissed her to underline the point he was making with Mrs. Crossland. Rachel knew that. He must have decided that actions spoke louder than words. If so, her response had signaled more about how she felt than she'd wanted him to know.

Too bad she wasn't in Dallas where she could escape to her apartment for a few hours to kick herself around the room until she solved the problem. That wouldn't work. She had chosen to leave her apartment—temporarily at least—because she no longer felt safe there.

At the moment there was nowhere she could think of where she felt safe. She grieved for her mother's wise counsel, not for the first time since losing her. She closed her eyes and tried to recall anything her mother might have said about her relationship with Brad.

Words began to form in her mind. As though Jillian Rogers Wood sat beside her in the Jeep, Rachel could hear her say, *Rachel, dear, I know you're attracted to your new employer, but you must remember how dangerous it is to get involved with anyone with whom you work.*

You are so right, Mom.

He's a very charming man, Rachel. He reminds me of your father in so many ways. The tone had been lovingly reminiscent.

The comparison had been apt and Rachel had reminded herself many times over the years that she wouldn't have had her mother's courage and strength of mind to make the life-changing choice Jillian made so young. She'd left a comfortable way of life and any contact with her family in order to marry Christopher Wood, the man she loved.

Rachel had vague memories of her father. Their home had been filled with photographs of him. She'd loved to listen to her mother's stories about him. Although her mother had been sad when she'd discovered the seriousness of her illness, she'd also commented to Rachel that at least she would be with her husband again.

Christopher had been a handsome man and, much like Brad, a self-made man.

When Jillian had first met him, he'd been working summers with a landscape crew to help pay for college. She'd been home that summer from the prestigious eastern university she attended, having finished her junior year in the spring.

Christopher had been three years older than Jillian, but because he'd had to work several months each year to pay for school, he'd only finished five semesters when they met.

Jillian loved to repeat to her children the story of how she and Christopher had met—how she'd spotted him working in her mother's garden early one summer morning, his bare, deeply tanned chest glistening with perspiration, his lithe, athletic body moving easily and without strain. How she had known that he was the man with whom she wanted to spend the rest of her life before they had spoken. There had been an instant of certainty about who he was and the effect he would have on her life, as though a voice deep inside her had spoken. *This is it, Jillian. There is the*

*man who will offer the loving relationship you've
wanted all your life. Get to know him. You won't be
sorry.*

Jillian came from a privileged background. Christopher had never talked about his family. He treated her like spun glass that summer, never touching her, rarely speaking. While he worked she would chatter on about school and her friends and shopping, but she never mentioned to him that she no longer accepted invitations to date.

She couldn't see anyone else, Jillian explained to her children. Her heart had made its commitment.

A week before she was due to return east, Christopher and Jillian eloped. Jillian had hoped that once her parents adjusted to the idea of her surprise marriage to someone outside their social circle they would forgive her and accept her new husband.

She'd been wrong.

Rachel grew up without knowing either set of grandparents. Her mother brushed aside any questions her children had about them, saying that it didn't matter. What mattered was the loving family their own parents had produced.

Rachel often wondered how their lives would have been different if her father hadn't been killed in an offshore oil-drilling accident ten years after his marriage to her mother.

Her father had taken the job because the position paid well and he had three young children to feed. He worked for two weeks straight and came home for an equal amount of time. Rachel could remember her mother's excitement when he was due home. Those were the memories she loved most.

She had been five when her father died.

The oil company made a generous settlement, but her mother had refused to use it for anything other than her children's education. She'd insisted that this was one of their father's goals for each of them because he and Jillian had never completed college.

Her mother struggled to make ends meet, but the children never felt deprived. In addition, they received a comprehensive education from their mother about how to get along in the world, a gift that was invaluable. Rachel watched her mother pick up the threads of their shattered lives and move on, making no effort to contact her family.

Rachel wondered at times if her grandparents had ever learned of her father's death. In the long run, their absence from the children's lives really didn't matter. Jillian provided for their needs, emotionally as well as physically.

As many times as Rachel had listened to her parents' love story growing up, she'd never believed that she was capable of throwing caution to the wind, defying her family in order to marry a man she'd only known a few weeks.

That is, until, all those years ago, she saw Brad Phillips standing in the doorway of a small café, obviously hot and tired and wearing clothes streaked with dirt and sawdust, coming to interview her for a job. In that blinding moment of revelation, she fully understood Jillian Wood for the first time in her life.

Remember, dear heart, Jillian had said to Rachel those first months she'd worked for Brad. *This is your very first position. It is important that you do well. Future employers will go back to this company for references and referrals. It wouldn't do to become emotionally involved with the man who pays your salary.*

It's too late, Mom, she'd wanted to say. It had been too late by the time he had taken her to his not-yet-finished office and explained that she would be expected to do the jobs of three people, her salary barely adequate for one.

She could have continued to answer help-wanted ads, but the thought never crossed her mind. She would take her mother's advice and not become romantically involved with Brad, but by accepting the job she would be able to see him every day.

Her goal was to help this dedicated—and lonely— man attain his dream. And she had. She'd long ago accepted that one day she would witness his marriage to one of the women he dated.

In her own defense, she hadn't stayed home and pined for a dream she couldn't have. She had dated occasionally. However, the demands of her job gave her the excuse not to become involved in an ongoing relationship. She knew that no man could take Brad's place in her heart. Most men stopped calling after she broke a date or two due to unexpected complications at work.

The thought of Brad brought her back to the present. Now she had complicated her life by giving Brad a glimpse of her feelings for him.

I know, Mom, I know. I've been a fool. But what do I do now? Resign and run for the hills? Pretend that nothing happened? Laugh it off as though the whole thing were a joke?

She heard footsteps and quickly looked around. Carl strode to the Jeep. She breathed a quick sigh of relief that it wasn't Brad. Not yet. Please. She needed more time.

He paused by the side of the Jeep. "You okay?" Carl asked, gazing at her intently.

She knew she glowed with embarrassment. "Sure. Why?"

"I saw you had your eyes closed earlier and thought maybe the heat had gotten to you."

She almost laughed because the heat had *definitely* gotten to her. Just not the heat he was referring to.

"I'm fine. Really," she said in her most reassuring voice.

Carl leaned against the Jeep. "Well, I think our silver-tongued boss has managed to deal with our client and her demands…at least for the time being."

"You must be relieved," she replied. In her panic she'd forgotten about the Crosslands. So much for staying objective.

"That was quite a performance you two pulled off in there. It certainly did the trick, though. Mrs. Crossland was all business after you left."

Rachel nodded, unable to reply.

Carl chuckled. "In fact, you should have seen *Brad*

after you left. He acted like a besotted lover too distracted to fully concentrate on the business at hand. It was all I could do to keep a straight face.''

Rachel cleared her throat. ''Do you know how much longer he'll be?''

As if he'd heard the question, Brad appeared at the front door of the house. He took the front steps two at a time and loped over to where the Jeep was parked. ''Sorry to take so long,'' he said when he arrived. ''I don't know how long it will last, but Mrs. Crossland agreed not to come to the site more than once a week. In return, I told her to check with her husband about her proposed changes and have him call me.''

Carl nodded. ''Sure. Okay. Whatever it takes.''

''Mrs. Crossland is lonely and bored, a deadly combination for a woman with too much money and time on her hands. I suggested she join her husband for a visit and see some of the sights of Europe. Who knows if she'll take my advice, but I hope she'll stay out of your hair,'' he said to Carl. ''If not, call me immediately.''

''Praise the Lord and sing hallelujah,'' Carl said. ''The miracle worker has done his magic again.''

Brad looked at his watch before he shoved his hands into his back pockets. ''Would you mind if I borrowed your vehicle for a while?'' he asked, his attention focused on Carl. ''I've got some calls to make, and the files I need are at the condo.''

''No problem,'' Carl replied sounding genial. ''When are you headed back to Dallas?''

''That's one of the decisions that needs to be made after I've checked with some people.''

Rachel looked at Brad in surprise. What was there to decide? He'd already told her they would leave in the morning, with or without a resolution.

With his eyes still trained on Carl, Brad added, ''I'll be back before you and the crew are through for the day.''

Carl shook his head. ''Don't bother. One of the men can drop me off later. With this problem taken care of, I may go out and have a few beers with the guys, shoot some pool, wrap myself around a big steak and do some celebrating.''

Rachel realized that if Carl wasn't going to be home anytime soon, she and Brad would be at the condo alone for the next few hours.

Oh, Mama, save me from myself.

Brad got into the Jeep without acknowledging Rachel's presence. He knew his rudeness was inexcusable. He also knew he didn't dare look at her until he could manage to control his response to her. His pulse still raced an hour after that sizzling kiss.

If he glanced at her he'd start to relive that moment…and to wonder about the obvious chemical combustion that had been set off between them. With his mind on what had happened he would probably drive off the damned road before they reached the condo.

They rode in silence most of the way back. They

turned into the entrance of the resort before he asked, "You hungry?"

"Not really."

"Looked like Carl had the kitchen well stocked. Guess we can find something there unless you want to stop at a restaurant."

"The condo's fine." She spoke with her careful finishing-school voice, a sure sign that she was on edge.

Well, hell. Why shouldn't she be? He had tiptoed around her for years, playing down his attraction to her, never allowing himself to face the fact that this one particular woman turned him on like no other. Until now.

So what did he intend to do about the mutual attraction the kiss had revealed?

Over the years she'd shared with him stories about her home life, about her dad's untimely death and how her mother had taken over the role of both parents. She hadn't needed to tell him that her mother had taught Rachel how to become the classy lady he knew.

Rachel didn't indulge in affairs. He wasn't certain how he knew that, but he did. Yes. Rachel was definitely a lady in the true sense of the word. He'd always thought of her as royalty. She handled herself in all kinds of situations with a polish that put him to shame. Always had.

Except that something had happened between them today, something he couldn't ignore. She had wanted him. He had felt the yearning, felt the heat…and had almost exploded with a sudden rush of frustrated desire.

He'd mulled over Rachel's problem with the creep who had left the notes. He had come up with some suggestions. She might not be open to any of them, but he wanted to discuss them with her while they had some time alone.

Carl had understood. He'd as much as said he would give them some privacy for the rest of the day and evening.

They arrived in front of the condo and left the Jeep in silence. Brad unlocked the door and motioned for Rachel to enter.

Once inside she hovered on the landing as though unsure whether to go down to her bedroom or up to the living room.

He nodded toward the stairs leading upward. "There are some items I need to discuss with you."

She immediately became his assistant, a role she played so well. "Certainly," she said. "I'll get my briefcase." She started down the stairs.

"You won't need it," he said. He didn't wait for her. Instead he stepped around her and loped up the stairs in three strides. Once in the kitchen, he removed a pitcher of iced tea from the refrigerator. After filling two tall glasses with ice, he added the tea and walked into the living room where Rachel stood watching him, waiting for his instructions.

Brad handed her a glass and gestured to a comfortable-looking upholstered chair. When she sat, he took the matching one at an angle to hers. He was close but not close enough to touch. Plus, he could watch her face and interpret her reactions to what he had to say.

She took a long drink before sighing with pleasure. "I needed that. I didn't realize how thirsty I was." She took another drink, which prompted him to do the same.

When he looked back at her, she'd set the glass on the small table between them and folded her hands. Her expression was serene, as it generally was. She'd reverted to her work mode, which wasn't what he had in mind.

"I have a couple of suggestions I'd like you to consider."

Slight lines formed between her eyebrows and she waited.

"Here's one of them," he said. "I agree that you shouldn't stay at your apartment. Who knows what this character might do next? You're smart not to ignore safety issues."

She sat back in her chair with a look of surprise. Okay, so she hadn't expected this conversation—this meeting—to be about her.

He leaned forward, holding his frosted glass between both hands, his elbows resting on his knees. "My idea is that you move in with me."

She stared at him as though he'd started speaking in tongues.

"It isn't as though I don't have the room. I do. You've seen my place. It's way too big for one person, but I liked it, I could afford it, so I bought it. It's secure, as you know...with the wrought-iron fence around the perimeter and electronic gates." He glanced at her before returning his gaze to his glass.

She didn't say anything. She just stared at him blankly.

"You'd be safe there," he pointed out, hoping he sounded reasonable and logical when he wasn't feeling either.

He waited, grateful that she hadn't immediately refused. Rachel generally weighed an idea, looking at it from all angles. He hoped she would see the logic in his suggestion.

Finally, she said, "You've given this some thought, I take it," in an even voice.

She acted as though being asked to move in with someone was routine, whereas his hands were wet, and not because of the frosted glass he clutched. He nodded, adding, "Since you first told me about the notes."

"That might be a temporary solution, Brad, and I appreciate the offer but I don't see where—"

"I don't mean temporarily."

She stiffened. "You can't be serious. I can't just move in with you permanently."

"Why not?"

"Because!" For the first time since they arrived, Rachel appeared agitated. "Because it wouldn't work, that's why. We spend most of the day together. We both need a break from work at the end of the day."

He nodded. "That's no problem. There are others things we can talk about."

That stopped her. A minute or so passed before she spoke. "Such as?" she asked, sounding a little breathless.

He raised his eyes and let her see how very much he wanted her. "Such as where you'll sleep, for starters," he replied softly.

He watched her struggle with the implications of his remark. "Are you saying what I think you're saying?" she finally asked.

He set the glass down and shoved his damp hand through his hair before he said, "We're two single, healthy people, Rachel. There's no reason why we can't live together, sleep together and work together." Did he sound as desperate to convince her as he felt?

"I can think of one," she replied after another long pause.

"What?"

"That isn't the way I choose to live my life. Up till now I've managed to conduct myself in such a way that I can face myself each morning without cringing in disgust. I see no reason to change."

He'd counted on that reaction from her, even when he'd half hoped she'd consider his suggestion. "I have a solution for that, as well," he said.

"Oh, I can hardly wait to hear this one." She dropped her head back against the backrest and closed her eyes. "What is this solution you have?"

"We can get married."

She lifted her head and stared at him in shock. She was probably waiting for him to smile, to make light of the suggestion, to insist that he'd been making a joke. Only he didn't smile. He'd never been more serious in his life. So he waited.

Her voice sounded tentative. "On how many occasions during the years we've known each other have you firmly stated that you're not the marrying kind, Brad?"

His mouth twisted. "Let's just say I don't know much about the subject."

"It's more than that and you know it. You've had ample opportunity to marry any number of women since I've known you."

"Yeah, but you see—I have this problem. I don't trust many people. Wait. Let me clarify that for you. I don't trust *anyone*. Except you."

"Oh, Brad," she said, sounding much too emotional for his comfort.

"Look," he said quickly, "you're my best friend. You know me better than anyone. Of course that may not be a positive argument for me to offer, but at least there wouldn't be any surprises."

"You're really serious, aren't you?" she asked slowly, her gaze searching his face.

He didn't like the tenderness in her voice. Nor the compassion. This was about helping her. He wasn't asking for her misplaced pity.

He knew what he wanted. He wanted Rachel Wood to live with him. He wanted her in his bed. He wanted her to be the last thing he saw at night; the first thing he saw each morning.

He wanted to hold her, to teach her how to make love to a man—how to make love with *him*.

"I've heard you say more than once that love between two people doesn't exist."

Where had *that* come from? "Yeah. So?"

"So what you're offering is a marriage where we meet each other's needs in bed, but we don't get emotionally involved. Do I have that right?"

He lifted one shoulder and let it fall. "I respect you, Rachel. You know that. And there can be no doubt in your mind after today that I can hardly keep my hands off you. I think our getting married is a much better idea than setting myself up to be sued for sexual harassment by one of my employees."

Brad felt the perspiration on his brow but refused to call attention to the moisture by wiping it away.

She nodded. "Ah. Yes, I can see the logic in your thinking."

He sighed, feeling a burden lifted from his shoulders. "So it's a deal?" he asked.

"No, Brad. I can't marry you, but I appreciate the kindness that prompted your offer." She pushed forward in the chair as though to get up.

"What are you talking about? I'm not being kind! I mean, I want to marry you but I'm not going to dress it up in a bunch of phony words that don't mean anything. What's wrong with that?"

Now that she had moved forward, her knee was touching his. He felt seared to the bone by the heat of her touch. He took her hand and said, "There's no doubt in my mind that we'd be as compatible in bed as we are out of it."

Brad reached for her other hand and pulled her into

his lap. Before she could say anything, he kissed her. He knew he'd made a mess of things, but he needed her in so many ways. She couldn't walk away from him. He had to convince her that they could make a marriage work.

Rachel shifted as though to pull away from him. He deepened the kiss with a hunger he'd been denying for years.

He lost his struggle with control when she responded to him, her mouth opening slightly while she slid her arms around his neck. She wants me, he thought triumphantly. At least she's not denying it.

Brad lost himself in the sensations that swept over him now that Rachel was in his arms. He could smell the light scent of her perfume, feel the velvety softness of her skin beneath his callused hand, hear her quick breath when he slipped his fingers around the buttons of her blouse and exposed her lace-covered breasts.

He dipped his head and tasted her skin just above the lace, nuzzling until he could touch the tip of her hardened nipple with his tongue. She groaned and gave a small shudder of surrender, causing him to smile.

It was going to be all right. He would make it all right. He couldn't go back to what their relationship had been before this trip.

When he lifted her shoulders, she helped him to remove her blouse. He paused and looked at her flushed cheeks and slightly swollen lips. He'd never felt such protectiveness toward anyone.

He unfastened her bra and tossed it away, at long last indulging himself in the sight and touch of her beauty. Once again he lifted her so that his mouth covered her breast while he stroked and caressed her bare back.

He found her mouth again, tasting her and wanting more. With long, drugging kisses that invaded and possessed, he placed his brand on her, making sure she understood that she was his.

Brad pushed her skirt to her thighs and rubbed his palm over the silk-covered curls. She was damp and ready for him. He touched her lightly, his fingers slipping beneath the thin material. She surged against his hand and made soft sounds beneath his lips.

He needed to take her downstairs to her bed—or his, it didn't matter. He wanted to show her how much he wanted her. He wanted to bring her to a screaming climax with his name on her lips as he buried himself deeply inside her.

Words she'd spoken echoed in his head...she wanted to respect herself. She wanted to be able to face herself each morning.

What in hell was he doing! Rachel deserved better than this. She was a lady and deserved his respect even though he had no love to offer her.

With a muttered curse he withdrew his hand, jerking at her skirt until she was covered. He pulled her hard against him, unwilling to lose all contact with her. Not just yet. She was boneless in his arms, her hands clutching him, her body quivering with need.

He felt lower than dirt, a new feeling for him. He

always took what was offered and eventually moved on. He could not treat Rachel so casually.

Not Rachel…his best friend…his only friend. He'd been truthful with her about that. He couldn't seduce her. He would hate himself if he did.

He gently kissed and caressed her, soothing the fire burning within her. He would not take her innocence. Brad felt a sense of shame that he'd momentarily considered seduction as a way to convince her to marry him.

He smoothed his hands over her shoulders and delicate spine, forcing himself to think about anything other than the woman in his arms.

When he eventually lifted his lips from hers, she had her eyes closed. Her mouth looked bruised, her cheeks scratched from the roughness of his beard.

He should have shaved again. There were so many things he should have done before taking this step.

She had every reason to hate him for what he'd done to her. Brad prayed she would be more forgiving than he deserved.

"I'm sorry," he whispered.

She lifted her eyelids slowly and smiled at him. Her small smile grew into a grin of such sensuous pleasure that it was all he could do not to grab her, take her to bed and forget about the consequences.

"For what?" she asked in a lazy, sultry voice.

"Getting you stirred up wasn't part of the plan. I don't want to seduce you into marrying me."

"How gentlemanly of you," she teased, sliding her palm down his roughened cheek.

"I guess I'm not doing any of this right. I should have taken you to dinner. I should have given you a ring—" *A ring! He'd never given it a thought.*

"Isn't that part of all the phony stuff you dislike?"

He eyed her uncertainly. She didn't look angry. She didn't sound upset. Instead, she looked as though she might start purring at any moment.

He wished he could say the same about himself. He feared that he would embarrass himself if he didn't get her off his lap. Now.

He lifted her, placed her feet on the floor and stood. There was no way to disguise his aroused state.

Damned if she didn't look fascinated by his condition.

"I'll be back," he muttered and stepped around her. As soon as the bedroom door slammed behind him he began to pull off his clothes. He continued toward the bathroom until he reached the shower and turned on the cold water at full blast.

What a ridiculous development, he thought as he stepped beneath the cold, stinging spray. He'd never had to take a cold shower to cool down from a heated sexual encounter. Why? Because he'd never stopped in the middle of making love, that's why. What was the matter with him?

Rachel was an adult. She was a woman who seemed willing to move to the next step. Why hadn't he taken what she'd offered? If he had, he'd be feeling a great deal less pain than he did now!

Still trying to protect her?

What a joke. He'd never felt protective toward anyone in his life.

He stood for what seemed like hours beneath the punishing spray, forcing his mind to go blank, concentrating on calming his body. He'd been an idiot to think Rachel would consider marrying him.

She came from good stock and pure bloodlines. He knew nothing about his parents' families, but from his observations growing up, he didn't figure she'd want her future family contaminated with any of his genes.

She was right, he thought, turning the water off. Of course she was. He towel-dried himself. It was a stupid idea. That's the trouble with thinking with other areas of the body rather than the brain. It got people in trouble.

He would get dressed and go apologize to her. Maybe she'd had the right idea before. It wouldn't hurt to take some time away from each other. There was no reason for him to think he couldn't get along without her. Of course he could.

Starting now.

He decided to shave, still cringing as he thought of the way his heavy beard had scratched her soft skin. *Don't go there.* He'd take her out to dinner, some place noisy with no atmosphere. There would be no dimly lit restaurant for them. *Don't go there.* He'd had a lucky escape, if he'd acknowledge it.

All that love stuff people carried on about might be all right for others. *But not for me.*

He dressed quickly. With a last flick of his comb

through his hair—he really needed to get a haircut soon—Brad strode across his bedroom, feeling in control of himself for the first time in hours.

He opened the door and came to an abrupt halt. Rachel stood there with her hand raised, ready to knock.

"Oh!" she said and laughed gently. "I almost tapped your chest."

"That's okay. Uh, look, Rachel, I know I was way out of line earlier and I apologize. I promise it—"

She placed her fingers lightly across his lips and said, "I just came to tell you that if your offer is still open, I believe our getting married would solve a lot of problems for both of us."

Why hadn't she just taken a bat and hit him over the head with it? She couldn't have stunned him more.

"Get married? You want to marry me?"

Her smile was as sweet as an angel's. "I believe I do, Mr. Phillips, I believe I do."

Chapter Six

She didn't look angry, which surprised him. He'd been certain that she would be furious that he'd taken advantage of her innocence by arousing her without bringing her to a satisfactory completion. He knew ways to do that, but he hadn't trusted his control…for good reason.

He continued to study her, saying, "Don't you think you need to consider my offer for a few days?" He felt like a fool for arguing against his own suggestion in an effort to be fair to her. He could think of nothing he wanted more than to marry Rachel. So why didn't he shut his mouth?

"If this was a real proposal, of course I would take more time but under the circumstances…" Her voice trailed off.

Well, if they were going to discuss this, they could certainly do it somewhere away from the bedrooms. He caught her hand and led her back up the steps to the living room. As soon as they reached the top of the stairs he let go of her hand.

He knew he was being ridiculous, but even being no closer to her than a couple of feet had a strong effect on him. He walked over to the sliding glass door and pushed it open, needing some fresh air.

An afternoon breeze wafted inside and he nodded toward the deck chairs. "Why don't we sit out here?" he asked, stepping out on the deck. She followed and sat across from him, her saucy skirt rippling in the breeze, reminding him of hidden treasures he couldn't touch.

He cleared his throat and said, "Now then, what were you talking about downstairs? My proposal is as real as it gets."

She smiled. "Perhaps that's true. I was suggesting that since we wouldn't be marrying for all the usual reasons, there's really no need to ponder the matter. I don't want to return to my apartment for any longer than it will take to move my belongings out of there. As you pointed out, I certainly won't be crowding you at your home. I think you've come up with a sensible and logical reason for us to marry."

He felt a strong sense of relief somewhere deep inside. His muscles relaxed, and he settled against the chair with a sigh. Then he frowned. Wait a minute. She'd been discussing the matter as though it was a business arrangement, using her professional tone—clipped and precise.

Brad studied her in silence. She appeared relaxed, leaning back in the chaise lounge as though content to enjoy the afternoon, the view and, perhaps, the company. She didn't look in the least businesslike in that colorful blouse and skirt. However, her expression was identical to ones she often wore at the office—calm and serene.

Hadn't his lovemaking affected her at all?

Of course it had, he reminded himself impatiently. She'd been as swept away as he had been. And yet...she showed no signs of frustration. There was something unfair about that. Did she have any idea how difficult it had been for him to walk away from her...physically and emotionally? Obviously not.

His mood shifted downward.

Rachel didn't appear to notice. "I suppose we need to decide when and where we should marry," she said, sounding thoughtful. "Do you have family you'd like to invite to the wedding?"

"No."

"In that case, I see no reason to make a big deal of it, do you? My family will understand when I explain to them why we're doing this."

He pulled on his lower lip before saying, "I haven't given much thought to the formalities surrounding marriage. I was thinking of the results."

"That's not surprising, Brad. You're a results-oriented person."

If the result was getting Rachel into his bed and

keeping her there for a few days—maybe weeks—then he could definitely agree with her assessment.

"Let's look at where. There's a three-day waiting period after obtaining the license in Texas. I don't know about North Carolina. I could go online to find out since I brought my laptop with me. If there's no waiting period, we could marry tomorrow before we fly back to Dallas. What would you like to do?"

She made the logistics of planning a wedding ceremony sound as if they were planning a business meeting.

He sat up abruptly. *So what?* he asked himself. *What was wrong with him?* He certainly didn't want a sentimental ceremony where they would pledge their love and devotion to each other.

Rachel knew him well. He could turn over the details to her and be done with it. "I don't care. If we're getting married, let's just do it, the sooner the better," he said.

She swung her legs over the side of the chaise lounge. "Let me check to see what would be most convenient." She went back inside the condo.

He continued to look out at the view. He wasn't as interested in the wedding as the honeymoon. Of course it wouldn't be a real honeymoon. They needed to get back to the office. Work was piling up. He wasn't sure it was a good sign that no one from the office had called during the past twenty-four hours. Maybe he'd better check in.

Brad went inside. Rachel was already hooked into the phone. He trotted down the stairs to his bedroom and picked up his cell phone. He hit the speed dial and waited for Janelle to pick up his personal line.

"Hello, Brad," she said with a smile in her voice. "How are things going?"

"I think we've managed to work out everything, at least enough for Carl to finish the job without needing psychiatric care. Anything unusual taking place there?"

"There have been calls, of course, but no one mentioned that there was an emergency. I explained that I could have you call them and each one said they'd wait until you're back in the office."

"Good." He thought for a moment. "Janelle, have I ever taken a vacation?"

"A vacation?" she repeated as though she wasn't sure that's what she heard.

"Yeah."

"Not since I've been here, but then that's only been five years."

"Point taken. Do you think the office would fall into chaos if I took a few days off?"

The smile was back in her voice when she answered. "I believe we could hold it together without too much difficulty. Rachel has always managed to deal with things whenever your trips took longer than expected."

He tugged on his ear. "Yeah," he said, frowning. "Rachel always steps in."

"Are you planning to get away for a while? I know it would do you good to rest and relax."

"Oh, you do, do you? And if I come back a changed man, do you think you can adjust?"

"Well, it's my guess that you won't be able to stay away for more than a couple of days. I can't see you lazing around on a beach somewhere without working up new projects and accompanying bids."

He laughed. "Didn't realize I was so predictable."

"Is Rachel still with you?"

"Of course. She's been a big help."

"I've taken a few messages for her—one from her sister who called to see why she wasn't answering her phone. I explained that she was out of town. I offered to give her the phone number there, but she said she'd wait to hear from her when she returns."

"I'll pass on the message. Put me through to Rich. I'll stay in touch. You know how to reach me."

"Sure. Hold on and I'll transfer your call."

After a series of clicks and beeps, the office manager answered.

"Rich Harmon."

"This is Brad. What's happening?"

He listened to a rundown of what had been going on and how Rich had handled everything. Brad was impressed. Rich seemed comfortable being left in charge. Maybe Brad could get away—with Rachel—for a few days without catastrophic results.

When Rich finished, Brad said, "We're leaving some time in the morning. I'll be at the office no later than midafternoon. If there's anything I need to review before Monday, leave it on my desk."

He hung up and went back upstairs. Rachel looked

up from her computer screen. "Okay, here's what I learned. If we want to get married in North Carolina, there's no waiting period. We'll need to pick up a license at a courthouse, which we can do in the morning. If we're lucky there will be somebody available to marry us before we leave. How does that sound?"

His stomach knotted. This was exactly what he wanted. His gut reaction was no doubt due to the childhood lectures he'd received about not letting a woman get her hooks into him.

This was different. If his dad ever met Rachel, perish the thought, he'd find his theory was wrong. Not all women were as bad as his dad made them out to be. Of course Rachel would have his dad totally confused. She was too honest for Harold Freeland to understand. His dad always swore there was no such thing as an honest woman.

Rachel would see right through Harold. At one time the man's charm and silver tongue had made him a great deal of money, but he would never have been able to con Rachel. She would see the hollowness that existed beneath the debonair facade.

There were times when he still dreamed about living with his father, following him from town to town, just ahead of the local police or sheriff.

"Brad?"

Right. She'd asked him a question, hadn't she? About getting married. That was the word that had sent his thoughts spinning.

"Sorry, I was thinking about something else. I believe you're right. Getting married here and flying back to Dallas in the morning makes sense. What do we need for identification to get the marriage license?"

"Our driver's licenses."

He nodded. Good. Once again his assistant had dealt with the details. He swallowed. "So where is the courthouse?"

"In Asheville. It really won't be out of our way since that's where the plane is waiting." She glanced at her watch. "I don't know about you, but I'm starving. Don't you think it would be a good idea to have a last meal as single people?"

His jaw tightened. "Is that the way you feel about what we're doing?"

"Not at all," she replied easily. "I was hoping to make a joke. You've been looking rather grim for most of the afternoon." She leaned against one of the bar stools. "Look. If you've changed your mind, I can certainly understand. I have other options. My plan was to go stay with my sister for a while. Once she got tired of me I could go to my brother's home. He has a large place in the country and I know I'd enjoy—"

"Whoa. You're really getting wound up and there's no reason. If you want to visit your sister, I don't have a problem with that. You deserve some time off…which reminds me, Janelle said she called this morning."

"Good. I'd left a message on her machine before I knew we were coming over here, giving her a heads-up on the possibility that I might be visiting her."

"Would you prefer to do that rather than marry me?"

"Are they mutually exclusive?" She grinned. "You know, Brad, you're beginning to sound like an anxious bridegroom with cold feet. If I didn't know better, I'd think that—"

"You know me well enough to know I always keep my word. I made you an offer. You accepted. We'll get Carl to drop us off at the courthouse in Asheville in the morning. We can get a cab to the airport later. Now, let's go eat."

Rachel was trembling with exhaustion by the time she crawled into bed that night. Brad had made a casual remark over dinner to the effect that she was one of the most honest women he knew. She hadn't been able to get his comment out of her mind.

She closed her eyes in pain, knowing how dishonest she had been with him today. At first she'd thought his marriage proposal an insult. He'd reduced the whole reason for their getting married to one of expediency. If she married him, his routine wouldn't be disrupted; if she took a leave of absence, he'd have to find someone to fill in for her.

Then he had kissed her so possessively that she had melted like a candle near a raging fire. She had never allowed a man such intimacies with her and yet she hadn't been embarrassed or shocked by his lovemaking. She'd reveled in it.

She knew that she would not have stopped the natural progression of the most wonderful lovemaking she'd ever imagined. The last thing she'd expected was for him to stop, when it was obvious that he'd been as affected as she.

He'd walked away.

Only then did it occur to Rachel that this man, who loudly proclaimed he knew nothing about love and had been adamant on several occasions about never getting married, was in the process of belying both statements.

His reason for marrying her was to protect her from a stalker. He had walked away from her to protect her from himself.

Her thoughts wandered through memories of Brad over the years. He'd been her employer and eventually her friend. To a lesser degree he had become her confidant as she had become his.

Few marriages started with such a solid foundation. She knew he'd taken the proposal seriously by his reaction to her agreement to marry him. He'd looked panicked at first before his jaw had clenched and he'd stood by his word.

Poor darling. He was scared to death of intimacy, the possibility of becoming vulnerable, and of sharing his life with another person. Despite all of that, he had stuck by his proposal. He was determined to do everything in his power to keep her safe.

If she hadn't been in love with him before, she would be now.

Brad was a man of honor and integrity. Of course she loved him. The danger would be in allowing him to see that love. If she wanted to witness panic in a grown man, all she needed to do was mention her feelings for him...which was why she was having trouble falling asleep tonight.

Somehow she had to maintain a casual attitude toward the whole business as though what they were doing was perfectly ordinary. Rachel had no idea if she was that good an actor. She knew she had to try.

She intended this marriage to last. There had been no talk of a temporary arrangement. They were comfortable with each other in the work environment and the small demonstration she'd received earlier that day hinted at a strong compatibility in bed. They had a foundation on which to build. She had to treat their marriage like a long-term project and have patience that someday—maybe—Brad would trust her enough to drop his guard with her. She would know when that day came, because he would be ready to talk about his life before she met him. No matter how much he insisted that his younger days were gone and forgotten, she knew differently. He still lived and made decisions based on his past...until today when he'd broken from the pattern long enough to ask her to marry him.

With that small encouragement, she knew she could trust him to discover for himself how his old beliefs had limited and narrowed any possibility he might have of finding happiness.

Chapter Seven

Brad gave up attempting to sleep and pushed back the covers. He'd been tossing and turning most of the night. He'd checked his watch every half hour since three, wishing either he'd fall asleep or dawn would arrive.

Now that the sky had begun to lighten, he would get ready for the return trip. Brad didn't want to think about his plans before they boarded the plane. He'd committed himself. He would stand by that commitment.

He refused to look past the ceremony. Rachel was far from a stranger. There was no reason for him to think she'd turn into someone else as soon as she became his wife.

My wife. He'd never thought he would use those

words. He'd sneered since he was a kid at the idea of being trapped by some woman. Brad felt that he had been the one setting a trap. So why did he feel he'd betrayed himself?

He stood in the shower and allowed the comfortably warm water to soothe him. He'd wear his suit today and the shirt stashed in his briefcase. He wanted to show Rachel respect.

He wasn't sure that marrying her showed her much respect. She deserved a loving husband and a family. He was incapable of one and against having the other. He knew there was nothing fair about this arrangement. He had all the perks lined up on his side—she would remain at the company and she would go home with him every evening.

She'd be in his bed every night.

His body immediately responded to that thought, which irritated him.

Brad turned off the water, dried himself and dressed, once again blocking his thoughts about the day ahead of him.

"I don't think you'll have any problems with Mrs. Crossland," Brad said to Carl on the way to Asheville later that morning. He stayed focused on the reason for his being in North Carolina.

"Hey, boss man, it was a stroke of genius to convince her she needed to be with her husband," Carl replied.

Rachel sat directly behind him in the Jeep. He couldn't see her, although he was fairly sure that Carl was communicating with her in some fashion through the rearview mirror. He was tempted to turn around and look at her, but couldn't think of a rational reason to do so.

She had gotten up early this morning and appeared fully dressed—in her suit, a new blouse and her office shoes—in the kitchen area not long after he'd poured his first cup of coffee. She appeared to be relaxed and well-rested.

He'd waited for her to say something to Carl about their plans, but she hadn't. He'd intended to tell Carl first thing but somehow hadn't been able to figure a way to drop the subject into the conversation. The very last thing he wanted was a big deal made over their plans. Obviously, Rachel felt the same way, since she'd given no indication that today was different from any other.

Now that they were on their way to Asheville, he'd expected to feel more relaxed. Well, he'd been wrong.

His dad's voice echoed in his head, voicing his contempt for marriage and all it stood for. Brad had grown up listening to his father's caustic and often witty remarks about the institution of marriage. *Who wants to live in an institution?* was one of Harold's favorite sayings.

Brad reminded himself for the umpteenth time that his marriage was more of a business arrangement. Even he doubted his own explanation. If this was about business, why did he keep remembering how Rachel had looked with her beautifully shaped breasts exposed to his gaze; how her mouth had fit so well with his; how supple and responsive she'd been in his arms?

More annoying than that, why had his body been in a state of semi-arousal ever since?

Rachel tapped him on the shoulder. He turned his head.

"Carl's asked you three times if you intend to contact Mr. Crossland, " she said crisply near his ear.

He glanced at Carl who kept his eyes on the highway. "Oh! Sorry. I guess my mind has already hopped ahead to Dallas."

Brad spent the rest of the trip to Asheville discussing some of Mrs. Crossland's proposed changes and how much they would cost. He found the discussion soothing until they approached Asheville and he knew he could no longer put off giving Carl their new destination.

Brad cleared his throat twice before he said, "We're not going directly to the airport, Carl." He recited the address of the courthouse. "Do you—uh—know where that is?"

Carl squinted thoughtfully. "It sounds like it would be near the courthouse."

"You know where the courthouse is?"

"Yeah," Carl replied.

"You can drop us off there. That'll be close enough," Brad replied feeling as though he'd been given a reprieve.

The three of them remained silent until Carl pulled up in a no-parking zone directly in front of the county building. "You want me to wait for you?"

Brad stepped out and helped Rachel get out of the back seat. "That won't be necessary. We can catch a cab to the airport later."

Carl gave him a quick salute. "Thanks for coming to my rescue, boss. I'll be talking with you."

Brad waited until Carl pulled back into the morning flow of traffic before turning toward the courthouse.

"You do that a lot, you know," Rachel said quietly.

Brad looked at her and frowned, wondering what he'd missed in this conversation. "Do what?"

"Rescue people."

"I wasn't rescuing Carl," he said, feeling defensive. "I was saving the project. This trip was strictly business."

"Ah," she said as though she were receiving instructions. "And marrying me is just another business matter, is that correct?"

He eyed her uncertainly for several seconds before he asked, "Are you offended?"

She smiled, her eyes sparkling with what he hoped was amusement…although he wondered what she might find amusing about their conversation.

"Not at all," she answered lightly. "I wouldn't want it any other way."

He attempted to cover his sigh of relief as he took her elbow and led her up the steps. Once inside the clerk's office, Brad realized that he hadn't given enough thought to the information that might be requested on an application for a marriage license, not until he heard Rachel giving her mother's full maiden

name as well as her father's name to the woman helping them.

He gritted his teeth and waited his turn for the in-
quisition. When the woman asked for similar information from him, he gave the answers tersely, refus-
ing to look at Rachel. As soon as they were finished
and the license had been issued, Brad asked the clerk
where they would find a judge available to marry
them.

They followed the smiling woman's directions, her
good wishes echoing behind them, and eventually
found the office of a justice of the peace. Brad explained that they were visiting the state and hoped to
marry as soon as possible. Whether because of his
nervousness—his hands were damp and his jaw muscle kept twitching—or Rachel's calmness, the justice
appeared to accept that they were serious about wanting to marry.

Brad was surprised to discover that the legalities of
marriage were simple and straightforward. They were
quickly pronounced husband and wife and he was invited to kiss his new bride.

He leaned over and gave her a quick kiss on the
mouth before thanking the justice for his assistance
and paying him for his services. As soon as they left
the office, Brad took Rachel's hand and strode down
the hallway, eager to get out of the building that
seemed to mock him.

Once outside, he paused at the top of the steps and
looked around. ''Thought there might be a taxi stand
nearby.''

"Perhaps we should call one," Rachel suggested.

He reached into his pocket and pulled out his cell phone. After connecting with directory assistance, he managed to get the number for one of the cab services in town, called and requested a ride to the airport.

While they waited for their cab, Brad paced. After he passed her for the third time, Rachel asked, "Is something wrong?"

Her voice sounded so normal, the way she always sounded—that hint of private-school polish her mother had passed on to her rounding her vowels.

He stopped in front of her and shoved his hands into his pants pockets. "I did this all wrong," he said gruffly, feeling like the worst kind of fool. "You deserved better than this. I could have gotten you a ring, and maybe planned some kind of party or something." He waved his hand vaguely, knowing he sounded ridiculous.

She smiled, that serene smile that invariably caused him to relax. "There isn't a time limit on buying a ring or having a celebration. We have time, Brad. You needn't be concerned."

"The thing is, I'm not sure how to break this news to the staff. We probably need to say something as soon as we get back, don't you think?"

"Why?"

"Well, I—uh—because they're going to know sooner or later."

"Then let it be later. Let's keep our private lives separate from our professional lives if we can. Until we adjust to living together, I see no reason to bring it to anyone's attention. Of course that's only my opinion on the matter.''

What a sane and logical way to look at a situation in which he felt at a total loss. He could let everything happen in an orderly fashion without making a bunch of decisions over a situation that appeared—at least in his mind—filled with potential land mines. Not the least of which was his having to explain to the few women he saw occasionally that he would no longer be contacting them. And why.

When he'd suggested the idea, he'd thought the marriage would be a simple matter, and already he could envision more complications than he'd foreseen.

The cab pulled up to the curb. Brad huffed out a breath of relief that his life was moving forward once again, even if it was only to the airport. He helped Rachel into the taxi, and only then did he remember that she really disliked flying. Not once this morning had she given any indication that she was bothered by the thought of the return flight to Dallas.

Rachel kept her emotions in check most of the time, now that he thought about it. She had accepted his suggestion to marry and he had no idea why. Maybe she was more afraid of staying at her apartment than she'd let on. Why else would she have planned to leave him—rather, the company—on such short notice?

He reached over and took her hand, smiling at her in what he hoped was a reassuring way. She looked a little startled when she glanced at him, but that was probably because he'd kept his distance this morning.

She might as well become accustomed to his touch. Although he'd never been much for physical contact—other than at the obvious times—he felt differently where Rachel was concerned. His problem now was fighting himself to keep his hands *off* her.

The cabdriver followed his instructions to the private part of the airfield where the jet and Steve Parsons waited.

Once he'd paid the driver, Brad picked up the small bag Rachel had remembered to buy to carry their extra clothes. Yielding to temptation, he wrapped his arm around her waist and strode toward the plane, adjusting his steps to her shorter ones.

"Mornin', boss," Steve said with a smile. "I checked with the weather service. We should have a smooth ride back."

"Good," Brad replied, conscious of Rachel's warmth beside him. He reluctantly let go of her so that she could climb the steps in front of them. He paused while Steve gave him a brief rundown of the plane's readiness after which the two of them walked up the steps. Once inside, Steve turned and prepared the door for takeoff.

Rachel had already taken her seat and was staring fixedly out the window when Brad approached her. He sat and took her hand after he'd fastened his seat belt. This time he felt a definite damp chill in her hand. She made no acknowledgement of his presence and continued to stare out the window.

Brad pondered the best thing he could do to help her relax. He'd learned not to tease her about her fears. He tried to think of something else that might distract her.

After a normal takeoff, the plane continued to climb to the designated flying altitude. Rachel had kept her hand relaxed within his, but the other one clenched the arm of her seat with such force her knuckles were white. Wow. She really had to concentrate to clench only one hand. Maybe his holding on to her *had* given her something else to think about.

He wondered if she wanted her hand in his. She gave him no indication either way. Brad realized that he wondered a great deal about her now that she was more than his assistant. He had no idea about so many things that made up the person he'd worked with for the past eight years...her favorite food...color...music...place to vacation or— *Let's face it, Phillips, you married a woman you don't really know.*

His father's knowing look of amusement flashed across his mind. He pushed it away and allowed his thoughts to wander without attempting to control them.

After the plane leveled off and the seat belt light flashed off, he lifted the armrest between them, unbuckled first his belt, then hers, and scooped her into his lap without warning.

She gasped and held on to his shoulders, her eyes wide. "What are you doing?" she asked, sounding more than a little breathless.

He grinned, suddenly enjoying a sense of freedom he'd never felt before. "Holding my wife for a while. Do you mind?"

Her gaze never left his. She seemed to be searching for something because after a moment she smiled and relaxed against him.

"Comfy?" he asked when she didn't say anything.

"Um-hm," she replied, her head resting on his shoulder.

He tried to think of something to say that wasn't related to business, but his mind remained blank. He'd never been good at social chitchat, but this time together—the first few hours of their marriage— seemed to him to be a time for sharing.

He could ask her questions, he supposed, but that might make her more nervous. He knew so many pertinent things about her—the important things, now that he considered it—that knowing her favorite food, color, music and so forth did not seem to be as big a problem as he'd first thought. No reason for him to get uptight about what he didn't know about her.

What she didn't know about him, though, might be upsetting to her if she ever learned about his past from someone else. Not that there were too many people who knew, but, just in case, he decided not to take any chances.

She was his wife now. For better or for worse. She might feel that she'd got the worst end of this deal, so it was better to tell her and get it over with.

"Did I ever tell you about my dad?" he asked, holding her close. He could smell the fresh scent of her shampoo and a lingering fragrance of her distinctive perfume. He rested his head against hers, feeling comforted by her presence.

There was silence after his question. A long silence. Was she too afraid to answer? He didn't want to continue talking if she preferred that they be quiet. Maybe that was just as well. For a moment he'd thought that it might bring them closer if—

"No," she eventually replied, her voice sounding a little ragged, "you never have." She didn't move except to slide her arms around his waist.

He closed his eyes, and immediately pictures of his past flashed by like a silent movie. At least most of them were silent. Lots of color and action, though.

"My dad was what's politely referred to as a con artist. That's a person who will sell you the moon at a bargain, guaranteeing to make you rich when you subdivide and sell lots. Of course, most of the people who bought his magical snake oil stories had to have a bit of larceny in their souls or else he wouldn't have been as successful as he was. You can't run a scam on an honest person, you know. For one thing, an honest person rarely falls for a get-rich-quick offer. He or she can generally see through the scam, rightfully believing big money schemes are suspect. My dad had a knack for spotting someone who hoped to get something for nothing. Those people who bought into his tales ended up getting nothing for something because my dad managed to pocket whatever money a mark contributed and head out of town in a hurry."

She hadn't moved since he'd started talking. When

he paused, waiting for the questions that were no
doubt flying around in her head, she tightened her
arms around him without speaking.

He held her more firmly against him, enjoying the
sensation of her soft curves pressed against his body.
Despite the unsavory story he related, he remained as
hard as a rock against her hip.

He ignored the urgings from that particular part of
his anatomy and continued.

"Harold never missed the opportunity to remind
me that there was no such thing as a free lunch...and
when something seemed too good to be true, it generally was. He bombarded me with advice as I grew
up. To hear him describe our life, a person would
think we were the luckiest people in the world. Putting down roots was for people too timid to take a
chance on life. According to him, he had the world
in his hand to play with as he pleased. He never mentioned the times when things didn't work out as he
planned."

Rachel rubbed his back in a soothing, gentle motion that eased his tension. Oh yes. He could become
addicted to her touch.

Brad paused to remember where he'd left off in his
story. "I need to give him credit for not abandoning
me, though. He could have easily enough. More than
once we barely escaped the long arm of the law because I slowed him down, but he continued to drag
me around the country with him.

"You see, my loving and oh-so-maternal mother
dropped me off at the motel where Harold was living

when I was almost four years old, then split, never to be heard from again. She'd been looking for him for most of my life…he explained to me years later in order to shut me up from asking so many questions about my mysterious mother.

"According to my dad, my saintly mom tried to pawn me off on some other john she'd been seeing on a regular basis when I was a few weeks old, but he'd insisted on a paternity test and was cleared. So she went after my dad next. It was a miracle that he'd hung around Chicago for so long. My dad, it seems, wasn't quite as lucky as the first poor sap. After being tested, he was forced to take credit for contributing to my presence in the world. As he explained to me when I was a teenager, learning that he was a father scared the hell out of him. He handled the matter as he always handled unpleasant situations—he disappeared as soon as he got the results of the DNA test."

Somewhere during his confessional, she'd paused in her stroking and pressed even closer to him.

"So, on that fateful day—night, actually—somewhere in rural Georgia, the woman who gave birth to me finally caught up with him. It seems she had contacts in high enough places that she had actually managed to track him down. He told me that she pounded on his door at four in the morning, bringing him out of a sound—and rather drunken—sleep. When he stumbled to the door and opened it, she shoved me into the room, together with a paper sack that held all my worldly belongings, turned around and left without saying a word to him or to me."

He felt her lips move softly against his neck. His throat closed when he recognized the light kiss she gave him. He waited until the lump disappeared to continue. He had never put his story into words before. He'd been too ashamed. Now that he'd begun, Brad was surprised to discover that relating his history wasn't as embarrassing as he'd expected.

Of course, the telling became easier because Rachel was the person listening.

"He said I bawled and squalled for days, driving him crazy, wanting my mother. I can never understand why I would have cried for her. Maybe I was scared of being with a complete stranger. My dad could have dropped me off at the nearest charity home for unwanted children, but for whatever reason, he didn't. Instead, he took me on the road with him, saying I was a great cover for him. Women flocked to the good-looking man with a dazzling smile and a little boy clinging to his hand.

"By the time I was ten he'd taught me the finer skills of picking pockets. He always laughed about that. He said I was the best he'd seen in the business. Yep, my one claim to fame.

"At least I was good at *some*thing. We moved around too much for me to stay in school for long. Most of the time he wouldn't bother enrolling me unless a truant officer happened to spot me. Harold was pleased when I reached the size where I could pass as being finished with school. I was tall for my age, which helped. He dressed me in his hand-medowns—expensive shirts and suits he'd acquired from various women over the years.

"I became used to leaving town in the middle of the night and heading for the next town in one of his various cars, if we were flush enough. Otherwise we took the bus. I remember one time the police were waiting for us as we approached the one-room apartment he'd rented. We were lucky they didn't see us, but we were forced to leave everything we owned behind.

"I remember being upset, but he promised me everything would be replaced and eventually things would get better. And they did. For a while. But never for long.

"And that, my dear lady, is a look at your new husband's rather shady—and at times downright unlawful—past."

Her hands stopped moving and she pulled far enough away to look at him. "Where is he now?"

He shrugged. "I have no idea. He turned up in Dallas a few years ago. I believe you talked with him. I wouldn't return his calls and I suppose he gave up. Despite the fact that he raised me, I have no desire to see him again.

"I must have been fifteen or so when we left Texas rather suddenly and headed to California. The bus made a late-night rest stop in Tucson. We went inside the terminal and he drifted away, looking for a mark. I'd waited for an opportunity like that for months and had saved as much money as I could. I bought a ticket back to Texas and hid until his bus pulled out of the station.

"I don't know when he discovered I wasn't on the bus headed for Los Angeles. He might have thought I'd boarded before he did and crawled into one of the empty seats in back to sleep. There's no way of knowing."

"You never saw him again?" she asked.

"Nope, at least not to acknowledge. I went back to Dallas because we had passed through there several times over the years and I felt comfortable there. Plus the winters were much better than in Chicago, which helped since I lived on the streets for a while. With my talents, it wasn't hard for me to get enough money to survive on.

"The greatest piece of luck I had in my entire, misbegotten life came to me on the day—about six months later—I tried to pick Casey Bishop's pocket. It was cocky of me even to try, given the man's size. He grabbed me by the arm and insisted on taking me home to my parents. At first he wouldn't believe I was alone and his disbelief devastated me. I've always hated being considered a liar when I tell the truth.

"Anyway, I guess I finally convinced him because he insisted I go home with him, which of course set off all kinds of alarms in my head. Who knows why I went? It wasn't because I trusted him. I didn't trust anyone. Maybe it was because he was so damned strong. Or maybe I was just having a bad day.

"Whatever the reason, I went. He lived in a spacious apartment in north Dallas. His wife had died the year before and he lived alone. On the way to his place he told me he was a building contractor, and he was always looking for good help. He asked me if I was interested in making an honest living or did I prefer living on the streets?

"He drove a late-model pickup truck and I remember actually considering whether we would have a wreck if I pounded him for that stupid remark.

"So Casey ended up hiring me and he meant business. He worked my tail off. He found me a small apartment. He hounded me into getting my GED and later going to college at night. He didn't understand how difficult it would be for me to enroll anywhere. For that matter, he couldn't list me as an employee for several weeks because I didn't really have a last name. Harold used so many that I was never enrolled under the same name twice. He'd make up some sob story about being recently widowed and that my school records would be following. We were generally gone by the time the school authorities insisted on documentation.

"It was when Casey insisted on putting me on his payroll that I decided to tell him about my problem. I didn't go into detail, of course. Otherwise, I would have put the guy to sleep with my sob stories.

"Besides, I knew he'd never believe me and I didn't want to go through that pain again. I just told him I didn't have a legal last name or a social security number. In fact, I didn't know at the time whether my birth had ever been recorded.

"Casey dragged me to see a lawyer—did I tell you how big that guy was?—who filed some papers on my behalf and got me in front of a judge who legalized my choice of a last name. I kept my first name because I was used to it. I took the Phillips name because I liked the sound of it. It was new and untarnished. I made a vow to keep it that way."

Brad felt drained—as though he'd been working at hard physical labor. He kissed the top of her head and added, "That is the story of my life and a great deal more than you ever wanted to know about me, I'm sure." He tried for a light tone but wasn't certain he'd managed one. He hoped for an equally light response.

Instead, Rachel asked, "Did you ever look for your mother?"

He snorted in derision. "You're kidding, right? Even if I'd wanted to, I didn't have enough information to locate her. The attorney hired an investigator to find my birth records in order for me to get my Social Security number. I gave him the information I had—her name was Mary Ellen, but I didn't know her last name. My dad never bothered to learn much about her. I calculated her current age because once, when my dad was drunk, he told me the little I knew.

"I knew that I'd been born in a Chicago county hospital on July seventh. I knew the year I was born, my mother's first name and that my parents had never married. With no more than that, the investigator managed to locate my birth certificate.

"Mary Ellen Ogden was the name on the birth certificate. The father was listed as unknown, which is really amusing if you think about it, since I never knew my father's real name.''

''So Casey was your mentor, in a way.''

''You could say that. I certainly looked up to him. He was an honest and ethical man—something I never believed existed until I met him. He became an example for me. I'll be eternally grateful for the fact that he never gave up on that belligerent, punk kid.''

''Where is he now?''

''Casey?'' He smiled. ''He retired several years ago. In fact, it was his retirement that pushed me into starting my own company. He made sure his contacts and associates knew me and knew I could be trusted. The business would never have made it those first couple of years without his help.''

''Where does he live?''

''He moved to Florida, became a fishing fool and fell in love with sailboats. The last time he called, he was thinking about sailing around the world.'' He chuckled, thinking about Casey visiting islands filled with sensuous beauties. Casey loved women. Always had. The problem was that his wife had been his one true love and he'd never considered marrying again.

Rachel leaned closer and kissed him, her lips lingering on his mouth, bringing his full attention back to her and reminding his body how much he wanted to make love to her. Brad couldn't believe the sudden effect his administrative assistant had on him, not after the years they had worked together without sexual tension.

He couldn't ignore the tension today. Her kiss was tender, something he'd never felt from a woman. It was all he could do not to strip her clothes off and devour her, showing her everything he'd learned about satisfying a woman.

That could wait, though. He didn't want to act like a barbarian, he reminded himself.

A thought flashed suddenly and unexpectedly into his head. He narrowed his eyes and looked squarely at her as soon as she straightened slightly from that all-encompassing sharing of herself with him. "Was that a pity kiss?" he demanded, knowing he sounded abrupt. He didn't care. He needed to know.

She looked startled by his words, and, after a slight pause, as though to catch her breath, she began inexplicably to laugh—peals of laughter that filled the cabin. Every time she would start to quiet, she would meet his gaze and convulse into more laughter.

"Are you laughing at me, by any chance?" he asked when she appeared to calm down.

She nodded her head vigorously, holding her hand over her mouth as though to stop another spate of sound. She appeared to be catching her breath. "I would love to see the expressions of the many women who have been in your life if *they* had heard that question coming from you! Honey, I don't know how to break the news to you, but there are lots and lots of reasons why a woman might decide to kiss you. Pity isn't anywhere on that list."

He stared at her in surprise. She had called him honey. Other women had used pet names for him—

names that had sometimes made him flinch—but he'd never heard Rachel call him anything other than Brad.

He smiled and pulled her close. She was right where he wanted her to be. Better than that, she hadn't seemed at all shocked by his story. Maybe he'd kept it bottled up for too long. Talking about his past had the effect of releasing a long-held burden. It no longer mattered what he had been and done in his past. What mattered was who he had become.

Brad closed his eyes and with a sigh of exhaustion and a new sense of well-being drifted off to sleep.

The quiet sound of the bell reminding them to fasten their seat belts woke Rachel some time later. She couldn't believe that she'd actually gone to sleep while flying! She raised her head and looked at Brad, who appeared sound asleep. She wasn't surprised. When she'd seen him first thing that morning he'd looked as though he hadn't gotten any sleep the night before.

Rachel moved off his lap and settled into her seat. Once fastened in, she reached over and fastened his seat belt as well, careful not to wake him.

She took advantage of this time to stare at him to her heart's content. She'd never had the opportunity to watch him sleep. The most obvious difference in the sleeping Brad from the man she knew was how much younger he looked when he slept. Studying him now, Rachel had a better idea of what he must have looked like when he was younger. The lines were gone from around his eyes and between his brows. His mouth looked relaxed and very kissable.

Pity, indeed. She grinned at the thought, but her smile soon faded. How could anyone hear about his childhood and not have compassion for the boy and be angered by the way he had been mistreated? He'd never had a childhood, that much was obvious. She also better understood why he didn't trust women. How could a woman abandon her own child that way?

She shook her head in disgust. It was a good thing she didn't know how to contact Mary Ellen Ogden. Otherwise she might be tempted to find her and yank her bald. Rachel couldn't remember a time in her life when she'd felt so ferociously protective.

She was being ridiculous and she knew it. Brad Phillips was one of the strongest, most independent men she'd ever known. He certainly didn't need her to kick butt and take names on his behalf.

How had he managed to survive such an upbringing? she wondered. Not only survive it but develop such strong morals and ethics. He certainly hadn't learned them at home. In fact, it was plain that the man never *had* a home.

Maybe God decided Brad had dealt with enough in his life and sent Casey as his messenger of hope.

No wonder Brad had bought the large house and acreage where he now lived. It was in a quiet neighborhood with secluded grounds. No doubt he'd needed such a place to return to after his day was over. What seemed so sad to her was that he lived there alone.

No longer, she thought. Brad Phillips would never have to be alone again as long as she had anything to say about it.

Chapter Eight

Brad awoke when the plane banked sharply to make its final approach to the airport. He opened his eyes and stretched before remembering that Rachel was with him. Rachel…his wife. Rachel…who was afraid of flying.

He quickly glanced at her. She had her eyes closed but wasn't clutching the armrests. Her hands rested loosely in her lap. He wondered if she was asleep. He didn't remember when she'd moved from his lap, but he'd felt a loss. He'd missed having his arms around her, holding her close. He'd never experienced such a yearning toward anyone and it unnerved him.

The wheels made a screeching sound as they contacted with the tarmac landing strip. By the time the plane had taxied to the hangar where it was kept and had stopped, Brad had unbuckled his seat belt and was gathering up his bag and briefcase, needing some kind of action to soothe this uneasy feeling inside him.

Out of the corner of his eye he saw Rachel stand and look around the cabin as though coming out of a deep reverie. When she looked over at him, she smiled, and Brad felt as though a large hand grabbed his heart and squeezed.

"You ready?" he asked Rachel brusquely as Steve walked into the cabin from the cockpit. She didn't answer but waited beside him for Steve to open the door. Steve stepped back and allowed Rachel and Brad to precede him. Once on the ground, the men shook hands and Brad strode toward his car, his mind focused on business, which calmed him somewhat. He didn't notice Rachel hurrying to keep up with him.

Business was something he knew about and felt comfortable with. Thoughts of his company soothed him as they always did. Suddenly he was eager to get to the office and return to his normal routine. He determinedly pushed all thoughts and feelings about his confession from his mind.

On the drive to the office, Brad concentrated on compiling a mental list of things he needed to do, starting with a meeting with the office manager. He didn't expect to hear of any crises that might have occurred since he'd spoken to Rich the day before. He just wanted to stay up-to-date on things.

Brad's mind settled comfortably into his routine. When they stopped for a traffic light, he realized that neither of them had said a word since leaving the plane.

He glanced at Rachel, wondering what she was thinking. "You okay?" he asked.

She turned her head and blinked. "Maybe a little groggy. I'm sorry I fell asleep in your lap. Your legs must have been paralyzed from holding that much weight for so long."

"Didn't keep me from sleeping as well." Then he brought up some of the pending work awaiting them, which they discussed the rest of the way to the office.

Brad had entered the company's reception area innumerable times on his way to his office, but today everything looked different to him. Puzzled, he paused and looked around. The colors appeared brighter or something…had the area been recently repainted?

He gave his head a shake. What was wrong with him?

Melinda, the receptionist, looked up when the door opened and gave them a perky grin. "Welcome back, Mr. Phillips, Ms. Wood."

He paused at the counter in front of her desk and said, "Would you let Rich Harmon know I'm back? Tell him I'd like to see him at his earliest convenience."

"Certainly," she replied, lifting the phone receiver.

On the way down the hallway he passed several employees who greeted him with a friendliness he'd never noticed before. Had they always been that way?

Nothing had changed to explain his new perspective, he was certain. Maybe it had something to do with the air pressure in the plane. He made a mental note to have Steve check it out.

He and Rachel reached the executive suite of offices. He opened the door and stepped back to allow Rachel to enter. Janelle looked away from her computer screen and smiled.

"Hi guys," she said, holding up two large stacks of phone messages. "These should keep you busy for the rest of the day, at least."

Brad nodded and went into his office while shuffling through the stack. He glanced around and saw that Rachel hadn't followed him. Instead, she'd gone into her own office. Maybe that was better. They could get twice as much done if they parted for a few hours.

When he had arrived, Brad intended to spend no more than two hours in the office. Instead, he was there almost four before he felt caught up on what had occurred while they were away. He went over to the door that connected Rachel's office to his and quietly opened it.

She was on the phone but saw him as soon as he paused in the doorway. She offered him a quick smile and a silent invitation to come in, which he did. He slid into one of the chairs in front of her desk and watched her. This was the woman he knew so well, the one with whom he felt most comfortable, the one who knew him and his temper and his impatience.

She knew all that about him and had still agreed to marry him.

He wondered why. Couldn't be because of his fascinating personality, he was certain of that.

He listened vaguely as she handled a rather difficult client with firm patience and no sign of irritation in her voice.

When she hung up, she raised her brows in question. "I'm wondering if there's anything there—" he motioned to the stacks of files on her desk "—that can't wait until Monday."

She rubbed her forehead wearily and stared at the mounds of work on her desk. "I sincerely hope not," she responded with a sigh. "I guess this is the kind of thing that *you* face every time you go out of town."

"Not usually, no," he said with a rueful smile. "You see, I have this terrific administrative assistant who takes care of most things while I'm away so that I can walk back in without a ripple in the routine. There have been times when I've felt redundant around here."

She chuckled. "Sure there were. Sorry, but I'm not buying that piece of blarney."

He raised his arms high over his head and stretched. After rolling his head slowly in a circle to release the tension in his neck, Brad looked at her and said, "I have a suggestion to make."

She leaned forward clasping her hands together on the desk. "Shoot."

"I suggest that we go home, see what I can find in the freezer to eat, and spend a few hours relaxing. How does that sound to you?"

The thought of the suggestion he wasn't making

must have communicated itself to her because a soft rush of color filled her cheeks. "You're the boss," she replied as her color deepened.

"Not necessarily in our marriage. I consider that more of a partnership. You get equal voting rights."

She stood and stretched. "Then I vote for taking off before the next client decides he has to get all of his complaints in before the weekend."

"Who was that on the phone?"

She told him, summarizing the conversation while she removed her purse from the bottom drawer of her desk. She straightened and added, "I think he's somewhat pacified now. At least I hope so."

Brad walked over to the door that led into Janelle's office and opened it. As Rachel walked through the doorway in front of him, Brad spoke to Janelle.

"We're leaving for the day," he said briskly, barely slowing down. "See you Monday."

Janelle looked startled to see them leaving together, something that rarely happened. Well, she would have to get used to the sight, he thought. He waited until they were in the elevator—alone, thank God for small favors—and pulled Rachel to him. Kissing her with a great deal of fervor, he reluctantly released her when they reached the parking-garage level.

"Thanks," he said, feeling lighter for some reason. "I needed that."

The elevator door opened and they stepped out, once again the CEO and his administrative assistant. He took her arm and gently tugged her toward his car. "I vote that we go directly home...we won't pass

Go, we won't collect two hundred dollars and at the moment, I really don't care.''

He almost laughed at her expression. She was no longer the administrative assistant. His kiss must have reminded her that she was a married woman who had her wedding night immediately ahead of her.

He gave her credit for attempting to appear casual about the situation. She glanced at her watch. ''I thought I'd go to my apartment first and gather a few clothes and items to take to your place. I'm too tired tonight to think about doing any serious packing.''

''You won't need anything tonight, will you? We can wait until tomorrow to go over there and I'll help you decide what you want to move and what you want to discard.''

She stopped and stared thoughtfully into his face as though she were meeting him for the first time. The searching look made him a little nervous. He wasn't used to getting that response from her. He wasn't at all certain what to make of it.

Her eventual reply caught him off guard. She gave him a slow, intimate smile. ''You definitely have a way with words, handsome,'' she drawled, kissing him on the corner of his mouth. ''I'm convinced.''

He laughed as they walked over to his car. He was holding her door open when another car pulled in next to them. Brad glanced around casually and realized it was good old Arthur from accounting. He was in much too good a mood to let Arthur affect him.

''How's it going?'' he asked, closing the passenger door and walking around to the driver's side.

Arthur got out of his car and blinked at him across the roof of the car. He pushed his glasses back to the bridge of his nose before replying. "Oh, everything's going along well, I think." He nodded to Rachel. "Hello, Ms. Wood."

"Hi, Arthur. Good to see you."

Brad slipped into his seat while Arthur walked toward the elevators. Rachel chuckled and said, "That's the first time I've seen you around Arthur without your teeth being clenched."

"For good reason. Not even Arthur can get to me today." He backed out and drove to the exit.

Rachel watched his capable hands lightly gripping the leather-covered steering wheel. She had always admired his hands. They were a workman's hands, callused despite the years that had passed since he was part of a construction crew.

She moved from that thought to another one. "How did you manage to learn anything at school if you were moved around so much?" she asked.

"My curiosity, I suppose. I remember being full of questions. Plus I really enjoyed school—the routine that other kids complained about I found reassuring. Because I knew I wouldn't be there on a permanent basis, I worked hard to catch up with the other kids and to learn as much as I could while I had the chance.

"Even when I wasn't in school, I'd look for the local library and go there to read whenever possible. Most of the time my dad never asked where I'd been. When he did, he always laughed when I said the library. I realized later that he thought I was lying to hide my real activities. He never did learn that I don't lie. It was a vow I made to myself when I was just a kid and heard all the preposterous stories my dad told.

"I didn't want to grow up and be like him. I figured an education was the only way I could escape."

"Your plan obviously worked."

"I guess."

She heard the aloof tone that told her he didn't want to discuss his past anymore. She was still stunned that he'd told her as much as he had. She had to respect his boundaries where his childhood was concerned. She never wanted him to regret having shared so much of his life with her.

When they reached his property, Brad turned into the driveway while he pressed a series of numbers on an electronic pad clipped to his sun visor.

Rachel sat up straighter, looking around as the gates opened and they drove between them. She'd been there one other time, when Brad had been felled by a virulent case of the flu and was confined to bed on his doctor's orders.

He'd complied with the letter of the instruction, but not the spirit. He'd called the office one morning and asked her to bring him some files. She'd suggested that he might want to rest for a few days but got nowhere with that argument. Thus, she'd come to his home and dropped off the files as instructed.

He'd given her the combination to the electronic gate, which he'd told her he changed on a regular basis. She'd had fun with the idea of having so much control over one's environment. No solicitors ever bothered *him!*

During that quick visit, she'd seen the foyer and living room of the house, as well as a grumpy, disheveled boss with a three-day growth of beard. He'd worn a robe that revealed his bare, broad chest more than he probably knew, and he, no doubt, ran a fever.

His voice sounded scratchy and he'd looked as though he felt miserable, but it would have done no good for her to suggest that he hire some nursing care while he recuperated.

She had delivered what he'd asked for and left. Now she would be living there. How strange was that?

Brad followed the driveway past the house and turned toward a three-car garage. One of the doors opened as they neared the bay. Once inside, he got out and came around to open her door.

She didn't know why she was more nervous now than she had been all day. She'd managed to hold herself together thus far. She'd been able to do so by blanking out the fact that today was her wedding day, no matter how impersonal the event had been.

"Come on, I've got the perfect thing for you," he said, taking her hand. His boyish grin caught her by surprise. She'd never seen Brad so lighthearted.

She knew her hand felt clammy despite the fact that she'd quickly wiped it against her skirt before taking his. Rachel followed him through the door between the garage and a large utility room that held a washer and dryer, an upright freezer and a series of cabinets that covered two walls.

Before she had a chance to do more than scan the room, he'd pushed open a swinging door into the kitchen. He paused long enough for her to see that the room had been designed by a person who enjoyed a well-laid-out place to work.

"This is beautiful, Brad," she said, awed.

"You like it? Good. My housekeeper comes in Monday through Friday. She prepares meals that she puts in the freezer. All I have to do is pop them into the microwave." He gave a gentle tug. "I'll see to that a little later. But before that..."

He let his words trail off as they continued from room to room until they reached the foyer, which she recognized. He turned down a hallway that seemed to go on forever before they reached beautifully carved double doors.

Brad opened them and Rachel couldn't believe her eyes. The bedroom was obviously the master suite, but it was the size that had her taking a quick breath. A basketball team wouldn't have trouble practicing in here, she thought, looking around.

The room had a masculine flavor with its massive furniture. A bank of windows lined one wall. She barely noticed when Brad dropped her hand and moved away from her. Rachel was too intent on seeing what the windows revealed.

She walked over to the middle one and peered through a beveled glass pane to discover one of the most beautifully kept gardens she'd ever seen.

The various bushes and flowering plants were laid out in such a way they resembled an English formal garden. She could see a couple of paths following the sloping ground toward the thick stand of trees at the back of his property.

"It must take an army of gardeners to keep everything looking so healthy and blooming," she said, turning back to the room, only to find it empty.

Where had Brad gone? She hadn't heard a door close. She listened and identified a sound she'd been hearing…water running in another room. Rachel followed the sound to a door that was open a few inches. She pushed lightly and it swung open to reveal a bathroom as large as her apartment bedroom. Golden faucets gushed a steady supply of steaming water into an oversized tub surrounded on three sides by mirrored walls.

She blinked in surprise to see Brad—already out of his suit coat and tie—checking on the temperature of the water. He straightened and turned to her. "Did you say something?" he asked.

"Uh, yes, I was just—uh—commenting on your garden…Brad, what in the world are you doing?"

"Preparing your bath, my good lady. I thought it would help you to rest and relax before we eat." He pointed to a shelf of bath crystals. "Add what you like to the water. Sarah, my housekeeper, brought those one day. She swears this aromatherapy stuff really works." He walked over to where she stood in the doorway and kissed her briefly on her forehead.

"Enjoy this while I find something for us to eat." He moved her aside and briskly left the room.

The thick towels were the same soft teal green as the plush carpeting. She saw her image reflected everywhere she looked. The mirrors made the room appear even larger than it was.

Rachel sat on the vanity stool and pulled off her shoes and hose. After shrugging out of her suit jacket, she unfastened her blouse, laying both items on the marble counter beside her. She quickly stripped off the rest of her clothes and approached the massive tub in anticipation. She chose a bottle of lavender-scented bath crystals and sprinkled them across the surface before turning off the water.

She perched on the side of the tub and swung her legs over. Tentatively she lowered her feet into the water and saw her reflection grinning back at her with delight.

The temperature was perfect. She quickly slid into the water, which came to her shoulders. Rachel had never seen a tub this large or this deep. She felt a guilty pleasure for being there when she knew that Brad had to be as tired as she was.

No wonder Brad would greet her in a relaxed mood and charged with energy after a weekend spent at home. Anyone would be able to recharge in this environment.

With a sigh of contentment, Rachel closed her eyes and allowed her mind to drift. This was just what she needed, even if she hadn't recognized it herself. Brad certainly knew how to pamper her.

She must have dozed, because the next thing she knew the water rippled around her in a gentle wave. Lazily she opened her eyes, then sat bolt upright when she discovered Brad lowering himself into the water. Since he was facing her, she had a full view of his well-honed, muscular body.

Her eyes widened further when he sank into the water and casually brushed his calf against hers. "Sorry. Didn't mean to startle you," he said, looking very innocent. She doubted that he'd been born as innocent as he looked at the moment.

Determined not to stammer, she waited for a few heartbeats in the hope that they would slow down before she replied, "I must have fallen asleep."

"I've done that a time or two in here myself."

The room had grown darker since she'd first come in. The indirect lighting, which Brad must have turned on when he returned, gave a soft glow to the ceiling and left the rest of the room in shadows.

"You certainly know how to a show a woman a good time," she said.

The slight smile on his face vanished. "You're the only woman who has seen this part of my home with the exception of Sarah, and she's old enough to be my grandmother." He studied her briefly before asking, "Is this how you thought I ended a social evening with a woman?"

"I wasn't thinking much of anything. Besides, I'm not asking for a list of the women you've dated over the years." *I don't have to,* she added to herself. *I know each and every one of their names.*

He floated to her side and said, "Would you like me to scrub your back for you?"

Calm down, she told herself. *Just because Brad's the first man I've seen nude, much less bathed with, there's no reason to freeze at the suggestion that he might come closer.* Wasn't this the epitome of the fantasies she had secretly harbored since she'd met him? Not even her imagination could have dreamed up a scene like this one.

Without waiting for her answer, he slid his arms around her waist and gently tugged her into the V formed by his legs, her back to him. She swallowed a gasp, afraid she was going to make a complete fool of herself. Now she understood the term *sensory overload.*

He reached for a nearby washcloth and a bar of soap and lazily stroked her back from her neck to the bottom of her spine. He made no effort to disguise his arousal, which caused her blood to heat and race through her veins. Feeling him gently nudge her bottom was another new experience, but one that gave her a great deal of pleasure.

She pushed more fully against him and was rewarded with a convulsive response. She might have imagined it, but she thought she heard him moan deep in his chest.

After completing the serious duty of running his hand over every inch of her back, he slipped his hands around to her chest, where he cupped her breasts.

He no longer made any pretense of bathing her,

which was just as well. If the cloth touched her now, it would immediately burst into flames.

She leaned against his chest, resting her head against his shoulder. She could feel his breath on her neck, or was it his lips that brushed against her? She tilted her head and he ran his tongue along the line between her ear and shoulder.

She shivered in delight. Her hands drifted downward to rest on his hair-roughened thighs. He tensed, and she smiled at his reaction. He gently nipped the tendon along her neck, then stroked the place with his tongue.

Her eyes had closed when he'd moved her closer to him, savoring all the things he was doing as well as her own responses. When she opened them she saw Brad holding her. Their reflections were multiplied in each mirror around the tub. She watched his face as he obviously savored her touch. She continued to explore with her palms, running them from his knees to his hips, this time knowing with certainty that she heard the deeply buried moan in his chest.

This was Brad, she reminded herself. Before this week she could never have imagined that she would be in such an intimate position with him. She wanted to savor every moment…but she also wanted him to do more. Her body throbbed and she trembled as he continued to play with her breasts—lifting them in the palms of his hands, placing his thumbs on her nipples and lightly circling them until they became hard.

She leaned away from him because she needed to

catch her breath. His hands dropped to her waist. With an ease and strength that caught her by surprise, he turned her so she now faced him, her legs on the outside of his thighs in a kneeling position.

He offered a beguiling smile and placed his hands on either side of her neck. "Comfy?" he murmured.

Before she could wrap her tongue around a sensible reply, he ran his tongue across the seam of her lips and, helpless to resist his touch, she opened her mouth to his possession and exploration.

Rachel lost the ability to think. She could only feel…and she was feeling things she'd never experienced. His lips and tongue seared her with their heat and she wanted more. She pressed against him, her breasts crushed against his chest, returning his kiss with a great deal more enthusiasm than expertise.

He didn't appear to mind.

When their lips finally parted, their heavy breathing filled the silence of the room. He pressed her hips closer to him, reminding her—as if she needed the reminder!—of his engorged condition.

When he touched her between her thighs, his fingers brushing backward and forward against her, she pushed down, causing his fingers to enter her. Oh yes, the relief of having him inside exhilarated her. He moved his fingers slowly and she came up on her knees and back down rapidly, signaling her need for more.

He brushed her mouth with his before trailing a line of kisses across her cheek. "I need to ask you something," he finally whispered against her ear.

She felt drugged, unable to concentrate on more than one thing at a time. At the moment her mind was fully focused on what his agile fingers were doing to her. *Please don't stop,* she thought. *Whatever you do or say, please...don't...stop!*

"Umm?" she managed to reply.

"Have you ever been with a man before?"

The question made no sense. Why would he ask about other men at a time when she—when they—

She opened her eyes and stared at him in disbelief. "Why do you ask?"

"Because I don't want to hurt you in any way. If this is your first time, I need to know about it. Now." His breathing sounded labored, as though he were in pain.

"Will it upset you to know that I haven't? I thought it was obvious that I don't know what to do next..."

He slipped his arms beneath her and with a mighty surge of waves stood dripping in the tub, holding her firmly against him.

"Don't worry about it, honey, because I do."

Chapter Nine

Rachel held on to his neck as he stepped out of the tub. He paused by one of the towel racks and said, "Grab us a towel, please."

She wrapped one arm tightly around his neck, probably cutting off his breathing. With the other, she filled her hand with a large towel and pulled it close to her.

When they reached the side of the bed, he eased her onto scented sheets. Sometime while he'd been gone, he'd removed the comforter and turned down the sheet.

He placed his knee on the side of the bed, took the towel and began to dry her off in a most sensuous way. He was teasing her past bearing. She reached for him, wanting to pull him down to her, but he evaded her move and rolled her onto her stomach.

She received another lesson in the power of touch before he straightened, rapidly drying himself off. When he stretched out beside her, she wanted to grab his shoulders and shake him. "Stop teasing me," she wanted to say, but couldn't think clearly enough to form the words, even though the feeling was close to overwhelming her.

He turned on his side and pulled her flush against him. She calmed a little when she realized he was as aroused as she. He was teasing them both. She didn't understand why, but she knew next to nothing about the act of making love. She knew the mechanics, which didn't begin to describe the emotions he evoked in her.

Brad kissed her gently on the forehead and her eyes fluttered closed. He kissed each eyelid before moving to her mouth. She surrendered to his tenderness, allowing him to set the pace.

He explored her with his mouth and hands, caressing her skin while he nibbled a trail down her throat. He shifted so that he was now above her, his knees between hers. Before she could draw breath, he leaned over her and caught one of her nipples between his teeth. The tension within her began to build.

He pulled the tip of her breast into his mouth and she arched off the bed in response. From her breasts he began a trail of kisses down the center of her body, his tongue sweeping lazily into her belly button before continuing its path. She stiffened when his lips reached the thatch of curls at the top of her thighs.

She reached for his arms, wanting to stop him,

wanting him to relieve her of this terrible tension that had taken over.

He ignored her reaching hands and began the same movements she'd experienced earlier, this time with his tongue.

"No!" she cried out, unable to bring her knees together because he was between them.

"Shhh," he murmured, placing his hand on her stomach and slowly massaging her while he continued to torment her beyond all reason. She could no longer hold on. She was going to explode and it would be his fault. If only...

She cried out as her release shook her body. Something within her exploded into thousands of particles, releasing a rapturous feeling that went on and on in rippling waves of pleasure.

Brad shifted and opened a foil package lying nearby, quickly covering himself before he eased into her. She tensed automatically at the unfamiliar sensation. He paused, and she forced herself to relax. *This is Brad. He would never hurt me.*

She slid her arms around his neck and lifted her hips, encouraging him to continue. She clung to him, wanting to express her love, wanting more without knowing exactly what she was seeking.

His movements felt controlled as he gently rocked above her. Instead of being soothed by his slow movement, tension started to build within her once again. She reached for him, wrapping her arms tightly around his shoulders.

He was slippery to the touch as though he hadn't

toweled off. Even his hair felt damp. The rocking motion increased until she could feel him surging deeply into her body. Unable to stop herself, Rachel wrapped her legs around his waist, receiving a low murmur of approval from him.

He lifted her by her hips, allowing her to fall back against the pillows while he quickened his pace, burying himself within her until she cried out once again. This time he joined her, his body convulsing deep inside her, while her inner muscles seemed to pulsate around him.

He rolled as he lowered himself to the bed, careful not to crush her. Not that she would have noticed at the moment. She was concentrating too much on getting her breath, which she must have been holding.

His breathing sounded harsh in her ear. She placed her hand on his chest and wondered if it was healthy for a heart to beat so fast.

He didn't seem concerned. He surprised her by leaving the bed and disappearing into the bathroom. She wondered if she should get dressed. They needed to eat. Perhaps after dinner they could—

Her thoughts were interrupted when he returned to bed, gathering her into his arms and holding her with a new possessiveness she found endearing.

She lay beside him, utterly content, her mind drifting to the strangest thoughts. How come no one had ever bothered to tell her about this transforming experience? she wondered. *Now I understand why the women Brad's dated didn't want to accept that their relationship with him was over.* What she had shared with him just now was definitely addictive. There was no question that she was hooked.

She deliberately forced her breathing to slow down. Rachel thought that Brad had fallen asleep when he suddenly spoke, his voice sounding gruff. "Did I hurt you?"

She opened her eyes. "Hurt me?" she repeated, wishing she understood why he would ask such a question. Men were definitely strange creatures.

He shifted and laid his hand across her abdomen. "Was I too rough?"

"Oh! No. No, you weren't. Not at all."

He slipped his arm under her head and tugged her closer. She looked at him with concern. "Did I— uh—hurt you in any way?"

She felt his chuckle start in his chest before it broke. "No, honey, I'm just fine. Better than fine, as a matter of fact." He lazily brushed his mouth against hers.

"I had no idea that I could feel this way," she admitted. "I lost all control. What an exhilarating experience."

He didn't say anything for several minutes. When he did, she was at a loss as to how to respond. "I had no idea that I could feel this way, either," he said.

What did he mean by that? she wondered. She knew very well that he had gained experience much sooner than most boys. Or at least she thought he had. How else would a man be so well versed in how to please a woman?

Well, she wasn't going to ask any more dumb questions. She would keep her eyes open and learn about him and lovemaking as quickly as she could.

Several more minutes rolled by before she gained enough nerve to imitate some of the moves he had made on her. She started by kissing him on one of his nipples. He'd had his eyes closed until then and she must have startled him because his eyes sprang open and he caught his breath. However, he didn't push her away, so she continued to replicate what he had done. She was pleased to see that not only were his eyes open, other parts of his body were waking up.

He kept catching his breath as she moved her lips down his body. *Okay,* she thought. *We'll give this a try.* She slipped her mouth over him, which caused him to sit straight up in bed. She jerked away from him. "I'm sorry. Really, I'm so sorry. I didn't mean to hurt you."

He grabbed her to him, hugging her tightly. "Oh, you didn't. I'm just a little sensitive at the moment. I—uh—think maybe we should get something to eat. I have a hunch I'm going to need energy before the night is through."

Brad opened his eyes the next morning to a room filled with sunlight. He'd forgotten to draw the drapes the night before. He looked down at Rachel, who lay across one of his arms and his leg.

He glanced at the clock and saw that it was almost noon. Not surprising, considering they hadn't fallen asleep until dawn. He smiled when he thought about what they had done to fill those hours.

He'd discovered a whole new Rachel last night. He would never have dreamed that beneath her proper exterior lurked a sultry siren.

Who would have guessed?

She was an enthusiastic lover. He wasn't certain he had the strength to help her move today. Not that it mattered. They had the weekend to sort out their separate lives and merge their belongings.

In any case, she would need to give a thirty-day notice on her apartment, so there was no rush. They would go over to her place some time today and pack up her clothes. They could deal with the rest of her things sometime in the coming weeks.

He rolled onto his side facing her and gathered her into his arms. She murmured something that sounded suspiciously like, "no more, please." It was a good thing she felt that way, he thought, smoothing her hair back from her face. He'd already performed miracles during the past eighteen or so hours. He wasn't at all sure he could continue that pace without killing himself.

His last waking thought was, "But what a way to go."

Brad and Rachel arrived at the office Monday morning at their usual time, before any other employees. Following their routine, they went to their separate offices to deal with mounds of paperwork left over from last week.

The problem for Rachel was that she was having difficulty focusing on the facts and figures in various reports. Her mind kept reliving the weekend.

She was still pinching herself to make sure she hadn't dreamed all of it. She couldn't believe how happy she was and how happy Brad appeared to be with her. She seemed to amuse him for some reason. Every time she looked at him, he was watching her with a grin on his face.

Whenever she asked what was wrong, his answer was standard. "Not a thing, pretty lady, not a thing."

She'd retrieved her car from the office garage where she'd left it last week. It was now tucked away in his garage. There had been no reason to bring both cars to the office.

There was a sense of security in being with Brad that was so wonderfully freeing she couldn't quite believe it was real.

They'd spent a couple of hours at her apartment yesterday. She'd packed her clothes and toiletries, but left the rest of her belongings—her furniture and furnishings—there for the time being.

The rest of the weekend had flown by as they indulged themselves in passionate lovemaking. She had discovered so many new and fascinating moods to enjoy, shocking herself with her boldness.

She'd acted on her suddenly frantic need to strip off their clothes and impale herself on him even though they'd been in the middle of making lunch. She'd learned what it felt like to awaken in the morning and discover her husband making slow, sweet love to her, bringing her to a sudden climax before she was fully awake. Their lovemaking had been erotic...and fun... and breathtaking...and soul-satisfying.

She sighed. And they had only been married for three days.

Rachel forced herself to work and eventually she was back into the familiar rhythm of the office routine. As the week passed, there were small changes in that routine. It was understood they would have lunch together, which had caused Janelle to eye them speculatively.

Rachel made certain she never met Brad's eyes while at work. She either kept them trained on her notes or focused on his ear. She'd already discovered that she had little self-control around him.

She thought she was the only one with the problem until Thursday of that week. After he'd been in her office to discuss a problem that needed to be resolved immediately, he'd walked out fully aroused.

She never looked him in the eye, it was true, but she had no problem gazing at the rest of his body.

Sometimes she fantasized about straddling his lap while he was busy with a phone call, or laying him out on the conference table and nibbling on him. She would have been mortified if anyone knew some of her more lascivious thoughts.

Rachel had turned into a total junkie where Brad was concerned.

Two weeks later Brad left home early and headed to the airport. He needed to check on a site in southeast Texas, but solemnly promised to be home early that night. He'd magnanimously offered his sports car for her to drive, but she refused. She had a very nice late-model car, herself. She hadn't been on slave wages for several years now, she'd reminded him.

Their farewell kiss quickly escalated and they were a little later leaving the house than planned. Rachel sat at her desk that morning, already missing the fact that he wasn't next door. She reminded herself that she'd often spent her day without seeing him. That had been before...before he'd taught her so much about what turned him on.

Her phone rang about eleven-thirty that Monday morning and she reached for it with a smile. Brad was probably calling to say hi. Just to be on the safe side, she answered in her professional voice.

"Rachel Wood."

"How about having lunch with me?"

The male voice, sounding nothing like Brad's, startled her. Then her brain kicked in, and she recognized Richard Harmon, the office manager.

"Hi, Rich. Is there a problem?"

There was a short silence before he said, "Maybe, but I'd prefer to discuss it away from the office. Let's stop by the deli, pick up something and eat in the park. I think the summer heat has cooled off enough to be bearable."

"Can you tell me what this is about?"

"I'd rather wait, if that's okay with you."

She mentally shrugged and said, "I'll meet you in the office lobby at noon, then."

"See ya," he said and hung up.

Rachel wondered what Rich wanted to discuss. Most of his contact with management was with Brad. Maybe something had come up this morning and he didn't want to wait until Brad returned.

When she arrived in the reception area, Rich was already there. He'd been speaking to the receptionist and straightened as soon as Rachel walked in.

"Ready?" he asked with a slight smile.

"Yes," she replied, continuing to the door.

They rode in a crowded elevator, stopping at each floor. Rich had a warm, outgoing personality, seemingly comfortable with everyone. Today he was more solemn than she'd ever seen him. Whatever was going on must be serious.

She waited until they had bought their sandwiches and drinks and had settled on a park bench before she said, "So. What's up?"

Rich concentrated on unwrapping his sandwich, taking his time before he answered.

Rachel had taken her first bite when he said, "There's a disturbing rumor going around the office, and I thought you should know."

She swallowed and took a quick sip of her drink. "There are always rumors floating around the office, Rich. You know that."

"I can deal with those. They come with the territory. This is different."

"Then tell everyone that no, Brad isn't selling the company, allowing a merger of the company or absconding with the employees' retirement fund."

He didn't respond to her attempt to make light of whatever he had to say, so she continued to eat her sandwich and enjoy being outdoors. Now that the weather was finally getting cooler, she intended to spend more time in the garden. Three men came in daily to make certain the place stayed well-kept. She hoped they would allow her to watch as they planted the autumn bedding plants.

When she'd finished her sandwich, Rachel tipped her plastic cup to get the last liquid from it. That's when Rich chose to say, "The rumors are about you, Rachel."

The ice from her cup fell forward, spilling out of the container and onto her jacket and blouse. She must have gotten some liquid down her airway because she began to cough, trying to get her breath.

Rich gave her a strong pat on the back and asked, "Are you okay? Can I do anything?"

She shook her head and continued to cough. He silently handed her his drink and she gratefully accepted it, sipping until her throat relaxed enough for her to breathe.

She handed him back his drink. "Thanks. There must have been a bone in that drink," she joked, hoping he wouldn't guess that her reaction had been caused by his words. She was a professional. She could handle the matter, even if the matter concerned her.

"All right," she finally said, straightening her shoulders and making sure there was no ice stuck in her blouse or jacket. "What's this rumor about me?"

Rich cleared his throat. "You know that I respect and admire you very much, Rachel. I can't deny that I was attracted to you as soon as I joined the company. I made my attraction obvious, pestering you to go out with me. You were very courteous with me and I understood your reasons for not seeing me away from work. Office romances can get sticky. You were right."

She wanted so badly to ask, "And your point is?" but restrained herself.

As was her way, she remained silent, knowing that most people were nervous when a silence fell. They tended to fill it. She'd been amazed at what she'd heard people say during such times and at their shock that they had done so.

"So," Rich continued after the silence had stretched to several minutes. "When I heard the rumors I did my best to squelch them. But now I hear that some of the employees are claiming they can substantiate the rumors."

"What rumors, Rich? So far, I haven't a clue what you're talking about."

"The rumor that you and Brad are having an affair," he said in a rush. "They're saying it started when you flew to North Carolina with him a couple of weeks ago and that since you've returned, you've been seen leaving the parking garage together on a regular basis. Some enterprising soul decided to follow you to see if he dropped you off somewhere, but he didn't. His car went directly to his home."

Rachel disliked the idea that she was being gossiped about, although variations of that rumor had been circulating almost as long as they'd had an office staff. She'd once overheard one woman stating to another in the ladies' lounge—neither of them aware of her presence in one of the stalls—that she was sure the only way Rachel had gotten the position of administrative assistant was by interviewing on her back.

She'd considered going to Brad with the story at the time, but by then she knew him well enough to know his temper would only make matters worse. He would probably have fired the woman, raising such a stink that everyone working there would have been *convinced* they were sleeping together.

She'd never been sorry for not confronting the woman. She had to consider the source and console herself with the knowledge that the story wasn't true.

This rumor could not be handled in the same way. She knew that. She also knew that she had been the one to encourage Brad to keep their marriage a secret. She wanted him to become more comfortable with their arrangement before suggesting that it might be time to consider acknowledging their relationship.

For the past three weeks she'd been living in her own world, a world with Brad in the center, barely noticing everyone else passing by.

Rich turned on the bench to face her. His expression was more than concerned. He might be apprehensive about speaking frankly to her. He might also hope she would feel guilty for breaking her own rules

about office romances. Whatever he hoped for, he was
no doubt disappointed when she said,

"Thank you for letting me know, Rich. I appreciate
learning about the talk in the office. It's never pleasant to be the one they're discussing."

"Don't I know it? I've happened to overhear some
tales about me that have curled my hair. If I'd bedded
half the women I'm given credit for, I'd be listed in
Ripley's Believe It or Not."

She smiled, gathered up her trash and stood. "I
need to get back to the office. Thanks for buying me
lunch."

He stood and looked at her, his expression sad. "It
was my pleasure, Rachel. I wish there was more I
could do for you."

By the time they returned to the office Rich and
Rachel were laughing about a remark they'd heard in
the elevator. She gave him a wave and went back to
work.

Rachel decided to surprise Brad by having their
dinner ready when he came home. Since they generally arrived at the same time, she hadn't had the opportunity before today. She wasn't sure when he'd get
home. He'd called when he left East Texas but said
he'd be arriving in the midst of rush-hour traffic and
she should expect him whenever he walked through
the door. He'd sounded lighthearted, which thrilled
her, and he'd made it clear he missed her as much as
she missed him.

She hummed as she worked in the kitchen, pleased

with how their relationship was progressing. She could see Brad dropping his guard more with each passing day. Not that she didn't understand why he'd protected himself for so many years. There hadn't been that many people in his life to trust. If Casey Bishop hadn't pulled him off the streets, Brad would probably be in jail by now. Or at least have a long record.

Instead he'd made a success of himself and his company. He'd learned what was expected of him in social situations, how to dress and how to hide his impatience...at least most of the time.

She heard the garage door open as she placed the large salad in the refrigerator. Dinner was in the warmer oven. His timing was perfect.

Rachel closed the refrigerator door and turned as he pushed open the swinging door. When he saw her he tossed his briefcase aside and in three long strides was beside her.

"Welcome ho— Brad! What are you doing!" she squealed, when it was obvious what he was doing. He'd picked her up and continued through the house until he reached their bedroom. The doors were open and he didn't pause until they were on the bed, pulling at each other's clothing, laughing breathlessly and coming together in a burst of impatient desire. All she could do was to hang on. Even after they'd reached their explosive climax, he continued to hold her and kiss her, running his hands over her as though to make certain everything about her was still in place.

Some time later she said, "I have dinner ready. Are you hungry?"

He laughed and sat up. "Starved, but I guess I'll go eat first."

They found robes and returned to the kitchen. While she set the food on the table, he told her what he had seen and done that day. She gave him a rundown of some of the problems that she'd handled and they were soon discussing company matters.

Later, after they had showered and were preparing for bed, she said, "Brad, I know I said we didn't need to tell anyone about our marriage right away, but it's been three weeks. Do you think we should make some kind of an announcement to the staff?"

He stretched out on the bed and pulled her to him so that her head lay on his shoulder and her leg draped across his thighs. "I've been thinking about that," he replied, idly playing with her hair. "The thing is, I feel you were cheated out of a real wedding. I was wondering if we shouldn't do it right—maybe have a church wedding if you'd like, invite your family and our employees and anyone else you can think of."

She lifted her head and looked at him in surprise. Never in a million years would she have expected such a suggestion from the man who had hired her eight years ago. However, she'd witnessed the changes in him and hoped they were because of her. She'd never said anything to make him uncomfortable about their arrangement. He'd been extremely careful to use protection whenever they made love, which she took to mean he didn't want children.

She could understand that as well. In time maybe he would feel more comfortable with the idea of bringing children he knew would be treasured and loved into the world. She'd already discovered that he had a wealth of love to give, even if he wasn't aware of it as yet. She wouldn't push him on the subject any more than she ever mentioned that she loved him. He'd made his feelings for her obvious. She didn't need the words, but there were times, when he was at his most adorable, that she had to bite them back.

"Hey? Did my suggestion thrill you so much you've gone to sleep?"

She kissed his chest, enjoying the sudden chill bumps that immediately spread across him. "I think your idea has considerable merit, Mr. Phillips. When were you thinking about doing this?"

He rolled to his side and pulled her flush against him, making it clear that he wasn't too interested in much more conversation. He slid his hand between her thighs and started teasing her. "Um. Guess it depends on where we decide to have it. Maybe by the end of the year. I want to take you around and show you off to everyone I know."

"I thought I knew most of those people already," she teased, catching her breath when he made a particularly audacious move.

"Probably, but not as my wife. There's some kind of an awards dinner around the first of December. I want you on my arm with your correct title. Think we can plan something by then?''

She groaned, unable to concentrate on his words when he was evoking such a tidal wave of feeling through her body. ''I'll get on it first thing in the morning, boss man.''

His last coherent words sounded like, ''You do that, pretty lady.''

Chapter Ten

The next few days seemed to speed up as Rachel kept up with her own work, attended meetings with Brad and set about the serious undertaking of planning a wedding.

Brad had spent most of the last four days away from the office. He hadn't flown anywhere, but he'd spent the week inspecting sites, meeting with clients and obtaining information necessary to bid on other projects. However, today was Friday and he'd scheduled all of his appointments in the office. He'd informed her that morning not to plan to get out of bed for the next two days. She'd looked him up and down and asked, "You think you're up to it?"

He'd insisted on giving her a sample of his staying power before they left for work.

Rachel had never been so happy. Her relief that their arrangement seemed to free Brad from his past couldn't be overstated. Unfortunately she didn't have a close friend with whom she could share her good news. She'd often been accused of being married to her job, which wasn't far off the mark.

She toyed with the idea of updating her sister on their plans but decided to wait until they'd actually chosen a date to alert her that she was going to be a maid of honor.

Rachel glanced at her watch. Brad had several meetings scheduled. He'd told her when he left for the conference room at nine that he hoped to return in time to take her to lunch. He was already later than he'd intended, but that didn't surprise her. Brad hated long, drawn-out meetings but there were times when they couldn't be helped.

When the phone rang a half hour later, she answered with a smile, knowing it was Brad, probably in a foul mood.

"Rachel Wood," she said.

"The intercom isn't working," Janelle said. "So I had to phone you."

"No problem. What do you need?"

"I have a message from Brad."

"Oh?"

"He rang through, told me about the intercom and asked me to call a repairman, then to let you know that something had come up and he couldn't make it to your luncheon appointment."

Disappointed, Rachel said, "Thank you for letting me know."

"Would you like me to bring you something from the deli?"

"Sounds great. My usual, please."

Rachel hung up and stared at the phone. His meeting must have put him in a bad mood if he hadn't wanted to take the time to call her directly. She hoped he'd be in a better frame of mind by the time they left the office that evening.

After lunch Rachel lost track of time until Janelle tapped on the door and said, "I'm leaving now. Do you want to lock up when you go?"

When she glanced at her watch, Rachel was surprised to see that it was almost six o'clock. "Sure." She stretched, suddenly aware of how long she'd been absorbed in her work. "When did Brad get back?"

Janelle shook her head and said, "He didn't come back."

Rachel fought to hide her concern. "Oh, it doesn't matter. I can show him these figures on Monday."

Janelle gave a small wave and closed the door. As soon as she heard the outer door close Rachel jumped up and hurried to the connecting door between her office and his.

His light was off. His office looked the same as it had when she'd checked it shortly after lunch. How odd. Brad had always kept her informed of his schedule and whereabouts since their early days, when she had *been* the office staff. She tried to think of a reason why she hadn't heard from him, but nothing came to mind. He carried his cell phone with him. She saw no reason why he couldn't have called.

She picked up his phone and dialed his cell phone number. After a few rings, his recorded voice asked the caller to leave a number and/or message. She hung up without saying anything.

Rachel had never known Brad not to answer his phone. He was too conscientious. Now she was beginning to worry.

Rachel returned to her office and put her files away in the filing cabinet. She picked up her purse and left the room, turning the light off as she went.

Once outside Janelle's office, she locked the door and continued down the hallway. Everyone usually left at five, so she wasn't surprised to find herself alone.

She met the cleaning crew in the hallway outside the company's doors. They waited for her to move out of the way and rolled their cart inside. She got into the elevator and out of habit pushed the button for the parking level. It was only after she stepped out of the elevator and saw that Brad's space was empty that she faced the fact he'd left her to find a ride home without the courtesy of warning her.

Rachel didn't know if she was more worried that something had happened to him or irritated that he could have left her stranded. Whatever had taken him away had better be of earthshaking significance, she thought.

She returned to the elevator and rode to the lobby. The security guard was already on duty.

"Evenin', Ms. Wood," he said with a smile.

"Hi, Sam." She looked out front to see if Brad might be waiting at the curb, but there was no sign of him. "Would you mind getting me a cab, please?"

"Sure thing." Sam picked up the phone behind his station and within minutes said, "It's on the way."

The longer she waited, the edgier she got. Maybe the honeymoon was over as far as Brad was concerned. Of course they hadn't actually *had* such a thing, but for whatever his reason, Mr. Phillips appeared to have forgotten he had a wife. This was so unlike him that she was stumped for a rational reason for his behavior.

The cab pulled up out front and she walked out of the building and climbed inside. She gave the driver Brad's address, sat back and tried not to be impatient with the heavy traffic.

Maybe the phones had been more messed up than she'd thought. Maybe he'd attempted to call and couldn't get through. Once she was home she'd probably find a message waiting for her. She comforted herself with that thought.

Eventually they turned onto the quiet street where she now lived. "It's the fourth house on the left," she said. "You can let me out in front of the gate."

Once she'd paid the driver, Rachel turned and walked to the keypad near the gate and punched in numbers. As soon as the gate opened, she stepped through and walked briskly toward the house.

Foliage screened the house from the road, a privacy feature she'd appreciated without thinking about the length of the curving driveway. Once she rounded the last curve Rachel saw Brad's car parked in front of the house.

Something was terribly wrong. What could have happened that he would come home instead of returning to the office? Alarm flashed through her and she ran the rest of the way, arriving breathless at the front door. Of course it was locked. She fished in her purse for her keys and shakily stabbed the right one into the lock. As soon as she managed to get the stubborn lock to turn, she rushed into the foyer, closing the door behind her.

"Brad?" she called.

There was no answer.

Maybe he was in the back garden…or he could be asleep. Maybe taking a bath. She didn't know where to go first. Forcing herself to take long steadying breaths, Rachel turned toward the bedroom wing. On her way there she happened to glance into the room off the foyer that Brad had turned into his office/den. She stopped, a chill running through her. From here she could see the top of his head over the back of his executive chair. He faced the garden.

"Brad?" she asked softly. "Are you okay?"

He didn't respond. Maybe he was asleep. She walked in quietly and circled the desk in order to see his face. She saw his profile before he slowly turned his head and looked at her.

She flinched at the look of hatred in his eyes. Hatred directed at her. She shivered. She had never seen that expression on Brad's face since she'd known him.

What had happened to cause him to look at her with such revulsion and disdain?

Brad lazily pushed the chair so that it swung back to his desk. Only then did she register the open bottle of bourbon sitting there. He held a glass in his hand. Without taking his cold gaze from her he turned up the glass and drained the remaining liquid in it. He finally looked away toward the bottle and reached for it.

The sudden chill that had swept over her when she first saw him continued to spread, causing her to tremble. The bottom of her world had crashed with a resounding bang and she had no idea why.

She returned to the front of his desk and sank into a chair. "Brad! What's happened? What's wrong? Did you get bad news?"

He concentrated on pouring bourbon into his glass. Shock turned her body to ice when she recognized that this wasn't his first drink of the day.

Her heart began to pound. Brad didn't drink. He might have one mixed drink at a social function but she'd never seen him drink at home. Nor had he ever done more than sip a glass of wine when they'd had dinner together at a restaurant. Her sense of foreboding intensified.

"Bad news?" he repeated slowly, enunciating each word as though tasting it. He appeared to review her statement carefully before he nodded sagely. "I sup-

pose you could say that,'' he agreed. His gaze fixed
on her once more.

She unconsciously leaned back in her chair when
she saw rage radiating from him. Rachel had never
been afraid of Brad, even when he stormed around
the office shouting about a subcontractor or supplier
not doing their job. He didn't do it often and she had
recognized that he needed to let off some steam before dealing with the problem.

She couldn't imagine being afraid of him, but she
had never seen him like this. She felt alarm at his
cold rage, not understanding what had happened to
set him off.

She clasped her hands tightly in her lap and asked,
''Do you want to talk about it?''

He studied his glass and the lone ice cube that appeared to be swimming in a topaz sea. When he raised
his head and looked at her again, all expression had
been wiped from his face. His gaze was shuttered.

''I suppose that it's necessary, yes.'' He took a sip
of his drink and leaned his head on the backrest of
his chair. With a mocking motion of toasting her, he
said, ''You first.''

He made absolutely no sense. Her fear and frustration mounted. ''Me? I do not understand you at all,
Brad. What do I have to do with whatever's upset
you?''

He mouthed the word *upset* to himself, shaking his
head with dark humor. Brad nodded his head slightly.
''What do you have to do with my behavior, you ask?
That's a good one, but I wouldn't have expected less

from you. You *are* female, after all. I don't suppose you can help being what you are.

"A daughter of Eve, good ol' dad would say. A woman lives a lie every day of her life, pretending to be loving and compassionate and kind. Especially kind." He took another sip of his drink. "You suckered me in, all right. I was the fool for believing you were any different from the rest." He toasted her once more. "My mistake," he added. "Won't happen again."

"You're not making any sense," she said, feeling as though she was in her worst nightmare, unable to comprehend what he was talking about. Daughter of Eve? Good grief. I wonder how long he's been here drinking himself senseless? The bottle is half-empty. He must have bought it today, which means he's seriously inebriated by now. She didn't need to strain her powers of observation to come to that conclusion.

"Of course I'm not making any sense," he agreed. "I'm just a dumb male, easily buffaloed, ready to believe anything and everything you feed me. All these years I never understood what a seductress you are, how cleverly you played me."

He leaned forward, his eyes burning. "Tell me, Rachel, did those anonymous notes that you so conveniently used as a reason to leave actually exist, or did you make them up so you could pretend to be afraid to stay? Doesn't matter, does it, because your scary story worked exactly as you planned. You knew how I would react when you came in to announce you were leaving, didn't you? You knew that I valued you as an employee and that I didn't want to lose your expertise. Well, lady, I've gotta hand it to you. You suckered me in without a struggle, and, like a typical mark, I never saw it coming.''

Rachel numbly stared at him. His obvious contempt and disgust shattered her heart.

''What is it you think I've done?'' she finally managed to whisper, tremors shaking her body.

''What I *think* you've done?'' he repeated in mock amazement. ''All right. I'll tell you. You set me up, lady. That's what you did. You created a scenario where you knew I'd do everything I could to keep you from leaving. Maybe you were surprised when I actually offered to marry you. I can see why. Hell, it surprised me. Of course it didn't take you long to jump at the unexpected windfall, did it?''

Brad leaned back in his chair once more and shook his head wearily. ''Well, I'm tired of the game, okay?'' He sighed, sounding defeated. Whatever this was had devastated him, she could see that. But what was it?

Brad's voice dropped. ''I don't know what you wanted from me. If it was money, you could have asked for another raise. If it was the opportunity to make me look like a fool, you've managed that as well.''

He swiveled the chair so that she could no longer see his face, but his stinging, painful words continued without letup. ''You must have been amused when I wasn't ready to make our marriage public. I played right into your hands, didn't I?''

"Did you?" she asked quietly. "What did I hope to accomplish by that, do you suppose?" She hurt so badly that she wondered if her heart had been ripped out of her chest. She much preferred feeling numb, but it was too late. Feeling had returned, much too much feeling for her to handle at the moment.

"I haven't quite figured out all the details, yet," he mumbled.

"No. I can see you haven't." Rachel stood and walked over to the window a few feet away from him. She stared at the garden as he did. She wondered what he saw, or if he was too filled with rage to see anything but red. "May I ask how you managed to discover this—er—scam of mine? Do you mind telling me?"

He continued to sip on his bourbon and stare out the window. "Not at all. There was no effort involved on my part. All I had to do was overhear some of the office gossip, which can sometimes be amusing…but not always."

She stared at him in amazement. "Are you telling me that all of this is about the rumors that you and I are having a hot and heavy affair? I'm sorry I didn't warn you but frankly, Brad, I never expected you to behave this way. If you don't want people to know we're married, just tell me to cancel our wedding plans, okay? All of this melodrama is unnecessary."

The sudden rush of anger felt good to her… empowering. Of all things for him to react to, she would never have guessed acknowledging their marriage would have been so traumatic for him. Just wait until tomorrow when he woke up with the grand-daddy of all hangovers.

He didn't look at her. He finished his drink and said, "Oh, it's much, much better than that, Rachel. Not only have you been able to get me to marry you but you've also begun sleeping with Rich Harmon without my stumbling onto that fact. I gotta hand it to you, lady. You're good. Really good."

This couldn't be happening, she thought. Brad had gone off the deep end because of a rumor? Because someone had seen them having lunch in the park? She gave her head a quick shake. She knew he had some strong trust issues, but this was too ridiculous to contemplate.

She straightened her spine and asked, "Where would anyone, especially you—who's with me ninety-eight percent of the time—get an idea like that?"

He dropped his head and began to mutter, as if to himself. "I've been so wrapped up in keeping this company going that I haven't spent much time on my social skills. I bet Harmon knows how to show a woman a good time."

Another wave of rage must have swept over him because he shoved his chair back and stood, glaring at her. "When were you planning to tell me about him? Or did you think you could continue to keep it a secret from me?"

Disgusted by the whole scene, Rachel crossed her arms. "I have never dated Richard Harmon, much less slept with him. However, Rich and I did have lunch together last Monday…a first, I might add. We decided to eat in the park, which no doubt caused all kinds of speculation among our inquisitive staff.''

Rachel prided herself on having a slow fuse, but the idea that Brad was making such wild accusations about her because she and Rich had been seen together set off the powder keg of her temper.

''I didn't know that you were in the habit of listening to office gossip. I would have expected you—at the very least—to have asked me about the gossip before believing it and condemning me as a liar and an adulterer!''

Brad sat in his chair looking for all the world like a hanging judge waiting to hear a puny claim of innocence before announcing his guilty verdict.

''Why were you having lunch with Rich Harmon in the first place?''

''I would just like to point out, Your Honor,'' she replied sarcastically, ''that being seen having lunch with Rich is a far cry from having an affair with him. Not that that seems to matter to you, Oh Righteous One.'' She paused. After taking a deep and hopefully calming breath, she added through clenched teeth, ''Rich and I had lunch together because we had business to discuss.''

''And this business that was so important couldn't be discussed in the office?''

''No, Mr. Phillips, it could not!''

He took another drink from his glass before he said, ''I'm really curious to hear your explanation about what kind of business discussion you were having that he needed to put his arm around you."

"His arm!" She stared at him in disbelief until she remembered choking on a piece of ice and Rich slapping her on the back.

Brad expected her to stand there and defend herself against his slimy accusations? To explain to him her innocent actions? Was this what marriage to Brad was going to entail?

Feeling a blessed numbness wash over her, Rachel said, "There is nothing wrong with your office manager and your administrative assistant having lunch together to discuss business matters. Where we choose to have the meeting is not your concern. However, as your wife, I no longer intend to dignify your questions by answering them." She looked at him with contempt.

"You once told me that you trusted me. Is this your idea of trust? It certainly isn't mine, and I do not intend to live under a constant veil of suspicion.

"You obviously have me confused with someone else, Mr. Phillips...sir...because *I don't lie,* despite what you were taught at your pappy's knee. I also don't pretend to have feelings I don't have. The only so-called secret I've kept from you all these years was the information that I've been in love with you since soon after I came to work for you. I didn't consider that a lie then and I don't now. I consider it self-preservation." She turned and walked to the door. Before she walked out of the room, Rachel paused and said, "Perhaps I should have remembered my mother's advice…never waste time arguing with a drunk." The look she gave him was filled with distaste. "I've wasted enough time since I got here. If you'll excuse me, I have some packing to do."

The tears didn't start flowing until she was safely behind the closed—and locked—doors of their bedroom. Correction. *His* bedroom. She entered the walk-in closet that was hers—he had his own—and pulled her suitcases down from the shelf. She gathered armloads of clothes from the racks and tossed them on the bed. Then she systematically emptied every drawer holding her belongings and quickly folded and packed them.

She found a large shopping bag to hold most of her toiletries. She kept her mind blank of anything but the mechanics of packing. What she had to do was to get out of this house before she broke down completely.

When she'd finished packing, she hauled her three pieces of luggage back through the house and directly to the garage, thankful the two largest bags had wheels on them. What she couldn't have packed, she would have thrown away. Rachel wanted nothing of hers left in the place.

Once inside the garage, she loaded her car, opened the garage door and carefully backed out.

Thank God I still have the apartment, she thought, following the driveway to the gate, which automatically opened as she approached. That's when she remembered that she had given notice to vacate the apartment. She had less than two days to decide what to do next.

Maybe she'd put her belongings in storage and fly to California, spend time with her family and evaluate her life and what she wanted to do with it. Thank God for family. They would put up with her moping around the house. They would also deliberately create distractions from her wounded heart.

An unwanted thought appeared. Brad had never known the luxury of a supportive family.

Don't start feeling sorry for him! she scolded.

If *anyone* deserved sympathy *she* did. Her fairy-tale marriage had just exploded in her face. Prince Charming had inexplicably turned into a fire-eating dragon, ready to burn her with his unfounded suspicions and ridiculous accusations. Where did he get off accusing her of cheating on him? Didn't he have one modicum of trust anywhere in his body? He hadn't bothered to check out the rumor. No, not Brad Phillips. He'd immediately jumped to the silliest conclusion possible. Oh, yeah, she was going to cheat on him. Right. The fact that they spent a large part of each twenty-four-hour day making love seemed to have escaped his very short memory. When was she supposed to see anyone else?

The man was crazy, pure and simple. She was certainly grateful that she'd found out so soon into their marriage. She'd get over him faster that way.

By the time she reached her apartment, Rachel had worked up a full head of steam, fueled by righteous indignation. Once parked, she dragged her luggage into the elevator and punched the number for her floor. As soon as she reached it, she carried her belongings to her apartment door, unlocked and opened it, before dumping her luggage inside.

After carefully closing and locking the door, she went to the kitchen and put water to boil for tea. From there she went to the bedroom and made up her bed with fresh sheets from her scented linen closet. The place had a closed-up feel to it. For good reason. She hadn't lived there in weeks.

What a close call she'd had. Her guardian angel must have been watching over her before she'd wasted more time and energy on planning a wedding to a blind, hardheaded misogynist who could quote his rotten father chapter and verse when it served his purpose.

Her tears continued to flow down her face as quickly as she wiped them away. Rachel ignored them.

To think she had believed her love for him would make a difference in his life and the way he looked at things! What had she been thinking?

She must have been crazy.

After making the bed, she returned to the front door, retrieved her luggage and took it to her bedroom.

Good thing tomorrow is Saturday. I can spend the weekend packing the rest of the apartment and getting ready to move.

Her kettle whistled and she went back to the kitchen and poured boiling water over tea. She felt full of energy. What she felt like doing was busting Brad's chops. He deserved it more than anybody she knew.

Brad lay on the bed Saturday, praying that he would die.

Very soon.

Before his next breath, if possible.

He couldn't remember ever having been so sick. He'd never been much of a drinker. Age hadn't improved his tolerance.

He'd been throwing up most of the night. Now he lay in bed with a pillow pulled over his head, trying to block all light from reaching his swollen and aching eyeballs. He hadn't pulled the drapes closed before going to bed last night and now he was paying for it.

His head pounded so hard he couldn't think. Hadn't that been the point of drinking himself senseless yesterday? Or maybe he'd thought it would be a good day to make a complete ass of himself. He should feel proud of himself—he'd done both.

Fragments of yesterday's debacle with Rachel had drifted through his mind each time he roused during the night. At the time he'd had no way of knowing if he'd actually said some of that stuff or merely thought it. Now he was fairly confident he'd said it.

A sudden memory of Rachel standing before him surfaced and he flinched. She looked furious despite her level tone. What had she been saying to him?

Brad groaned. He wasn't at all sure he was ready to remember.

He couldn't recall when last night he'd realized that Rachel wasn't in bed with him. She must really be mad at him to have gone to bed in one of the guest rooms.

Just as well. He didn't want anyone seeing him like this.

He barely remembered yesterday evening, and the night—except for being so sick—was a total blank. What stood out clearly in his mind was the conversation he'd overheard at the office.

He'd gone to Arthur's office to get a copy of a report he'd misplaced. When he found the office empty, he decided to leave a note on the desk. He seldom came into this part of the office, and he didn't recognize the male and female voices talking in the hall. He continued to write the note while he absently tuned into the conversation.

The woman said, "And did you see her out in the park with Rich on Monday? They couldn't keep their hands off each other. I saw him with his arm around her, holding a drink to her mouth like she was helpless or something."

The words didn't register until the man replied, "I wonder what the prim Ms. Wood hopes to gain from keeping Rich's bed warm these days? You knew she moved in with the boss, didn't you?"

Brad stiffened, realizing the discussion was about Rachel. Rachel and Rich Harmon. What the hell was that about?

"No!" the woman was saying. "How did you hear that?"

The man laughed. "It's common knowledge. Why do you think the boss took her with him on his last trip? She must be highly addictive!"

"Well," the woman replied with a sniff, "All I know is that from the way Rich was pawing her, I'd guess she's seen the color of his sheets more than once. I could scarcely believe my eyes. Right there in the park where everyone could see them. Talk about brazen behavior."

Brad couldn't move. The unknown couple continued down the hallway, unaware that they had just ripped his life apart.

The stupidity of his reaction now galled him. However, at the time he hadn't doubted what he'd heard. He'd always thought that Rachel was too good for him, had always been afraid he wouldn't be able to hold her.

He remembered wondering how long Harmon had pursued Rachel. Rich had quite a reputation for being a ladies' man. Rachel was inexperienced. Harmon must have taken advantage of that.

Or so he had stupidly thought at the time.

He'd been on his way back to meet Rachel for lunch when he'd stopped at Arthur's office. He was too upset to face her then. He'd called Janelle, canceled his afternoon appointments and had left the office.

From that point on, his memory grew hazy. He vaguely recalled stopping at a liquor store and buying a bottle of bourbon. Why bourbon, he now wondered? He'd never liked the stuff.

For good reason, his abused body reminded him.

The next thing he recalled was sitting in his office at home, staring out at the garden and thinking. All right, brooding. He'd wondered why he had thought Rachel would be any different from every other woman he'd known. He'd watched his dad seduce women from their husbands for years. He knew how easily it could be done.

But not Rachel! his mind screamed at him now. Never Rachel. Rachel loved him.

Where had *that* come from?

Rachel loved him…she had said so, hadn't she? He thought he remembered that part. She hadn't sounded too happy about it, though.

He rolled to his side in an effort to sit up and immediately regretted it. He closed his eyes, still clutching the pillow, and prayed for his imminent death.

Holding the pillow soothed him. It carried Rachel's light scent. Even though she had refused to sleep with him last night—for good reason, considering some of the memories that continued to seep into his mind— he could at least hold her pillow for reassurance.

He forced his eyes open and stared at the open closet door, remembering how he had cried yesterday. Had he cried in front of Rachel? Dear lord, he hoped not. That would really have impressed her.

Slowly his eyes focused on the interior of the closet—Rachel's walk-in closet. Rachel's *empty* walk-in closet.

The shock brought him upright.

"Rachel?" he croaked. He waited, but heard nothing. Speaking increased the pounding in his head. Why would she have taken her clothes out of the closet? What had he said to her?

He sat on the side of the bed and held his head so that the damn thing wouldn't roll off his shoulders. What had he *said* to her?

He'd accused her of having an affair with Harmon; that's what he'd done. He didn't know whether to laugh or to cry. Rachel? His Rachel? What an idiotic thing to say…to believe for more than a split second….

But he'd believed it, hadn't he? Of course he had. That's why he'd bought the bottle and come home to wallow in his misery and pain. The thought of anyone holding her, even in a public park, had devastated him.

That part had been true, though, hadn't it? She'd said something about meeting Rich for lunch in the park. That was odd behavior for Rachel, wasn't it?

Wasn't it?

He couldn't think and his empty stomach continued to protest its treatment.

Brad pushed himself to his feet and managed to walk to the window, where he carefully pulled the drapes closed. *Blessed relief,* he thought.

He had to find Rachel and apologize for his behavior. She had every right to be furious with him. Absolutely furious. He would need to grovel—which he was fully prepared to do—but it might be better if he got himself cleaned up some first. He'd just discovered he'd slept—what little sleep he'd gotten—in his clothes last night.

He reluctantly released Rachel's pillow and managed to make it to the bathroom without stumbling. He stripped and stepped into the shower, letting the water beat down on his head. He'd either drown or his head would clear. He didn't particularly care which.

Brad tried to remember what helped a hangover, but the only thing that came to mind was his dad's phrase...the hair of the dog...which would never work. He strongly doubted that he would ever be able to smell bourbon without barfing.

Eventually he dried off and pulled on a ratty pair of jeans and a shirt with the sleeves ripped out. Feeling almost like a functioning human being once more, he went in search of Rachel.

She was nowhere to be found. Walking carefully in order to keep his balance and make the least amount of noise to protect his aching head, Brad retraced his steps to their bedroom. Her closet was stripped bare.

Her toiletries were gone from the bathroom. He hadn't noticed that earlier. He opened a few drawers and knew he'd find them empty.

Rachel had left him.

He had to do something. He couldn't let her leave without explaining his behavior. His thoughts were in turmoil and his head continued to throb.

First things first. He went to the kitchen and made a pot of very strong coffee.

By the third cup, his brain kicked in and his morale dropped to zero.

Had he really said all those disgusting things to her? Well, of course he had. Had he expected her to stay and listen to his insane tirade? Of course not.

What happened now? he wondered. What if she refused to have anything more to do with him? He couldn't imagine life without Rachel.

They'd been married for only four weeks, but she'd been a part of his life for much longer than that—a necessary part. As necessary to him as the air he breathed and the food he ate.

Why had he never faced that fact before now?

Everything he'd ever wanted or thought he'd needed while growing up had either been taken away from him or denied him. What had happened to the dreams of that young boy?

His most secret desire back then had been to be a part of a whole family, one with a husband and a wife, one with sons and daughters to love and to hold. He'd wanted to belong to someone. To belong somewhere.

To be loved.

Rachel had given him a sense of home. The company had been their baby. He'd taken on the role of daddy going off to job sites each day while Rachel had stayed at home—or in their case the office. She'd brought order to the place and made sure everything ran smoothly.

Rachel had been the one to tell him when to hire

more staff, who convinced him to move their office to its present location. He'd worked to bring in the income. She had taken care of the rest.

He'd been married to Rachel for years and never realized it until now.

He'd been in love with Rachel for years and never realized it.

Until now.

Dear God, what had he done?

He'd made unspeakable accusations. Panicked that he might lose her, he'd done and said everything in his power to drive her away.

He'd been successful; that was obvious. Now he wondered how he was going to survive without her.

Brad poured the last of the coffee in his cup and put some bread in the toaster. He had to do something to overcome the alcohol poisoning.

By the time he finished his meager breakfast, he knew what he had to do.

He had to find Rachel. As soon as possible. She'd planned to leave town before, maybe she had decided to follow through with her plans.

If so, she must have gone to her apartment. They had planned to move her furniture and clear out the apartment this weekend. He looked at his watch and groaned. It was almost three o'clock. He had no idea when she had left the house.

What if she'd already left town?

He had to find her...even if he had to follow her from here to California.

* * *

Rachel stood on a chair at the back of her closet, pulling stored Christmas ornaments down. She'd been working since she'd gotten up this morning. She hadn't slept much last night. When she *had* slept she'd had nightmares—hooded figures chasing her down dark alleyways, Brad accusing her of embezzling from the firm one time, testifying against her at her witch trial another time. She'd been exhausted when she'd finally dragged herself out of bed this morning.

Since then she'd made a great deal of progress on the apartment. Most of the kitchen was packed. She'd gone out earlier and got boxes from a nearby supermarket. She'd looked in the yellow pages for storage units and a moving company that handled local moves.

Regardless of how she felt, she had continued to function. She would get through this. She had no doubt she'd survive. What caused her to tear up from time to time was the realization that these last few weeks had been a mirage and not real at all. Was it only a few days ago when she'd been looking forward to starting a family? How could she have been so deluded?

Rachel stepped down from the chair and carried the boxes out to her bedroom. The room was beginning to look like a storage room. She could scarcely see the bed for the boxes.

The doorbell startled her. She certainly wasn't expecting visitors. Who would know she was here? She shivered. Her stalker might. Or maybe she'd made him up, as Brad had suggested. Maybe she was such a deluded spinster that she'd imagined the notes in order to gain attention. No one else had taken them seriously.

The doorbell rang again and she wondered if she had finally gone over the edge. Instead of speculating on who it might be, she could go to the door and find out.

"Coming," she said, winding her way through the boxes that now littered her apartment. She paused to look through the security hole, hoping to recognize whoever it was.

When she did, she let out her breath. She had no idea what he was doing here, but she supposed she would soon find out.

She unlatched the door and opened it. "What a surprise. Come on in."

Chapter Eleven

Arthur Simmons smiled sheepishly at Rachel and said, "I'm sorry for dropping in on you like this. I hope you don't mind." He nervously pushed his glasses back up the bridge of his nose. He looked at her with concern and she remembered that her eyes were so swollen they looked like slits. If he asked, she'd mumble something about allergies and change the subject.

Rachel was actually pleased to see him. He would distract her from the thoughts running around in her head like gerbils on a wheel.

She reached out and took his hand. "I don't mind at all, Arthur. Please, come in and keep me company, if you can stand the mess."

He accepted her hand and stepped into the apartment.

"Would you like something to drink? Coffee? Tea? I may have some soft drinks in the pantry."

"Oh, I don't want to put you to any trouble. Really. I wanted to speak to you about something and I felt it would be better not to discuss the matter at the office."

She released his hand and closed the door, motioning him into the living room. She wanted to roll her eyes but didn't dare in case he caught her. There was no reason to hurt his feelings. There was no doubt in Rachel's mind that Arthur was here because he intended to discuss how her reputation was being shredded at the office.

Her reputation no longer bothered her. It was her shredded heart that might not recover.

"It's no trouble." She walked into the small kitchen and looked at him over the bar. "Have a seat and I'll get you whatever you'd like." She opened her pantry door and smiled. "I have several choices for soft drinks. It depends on whether you want something hot or something cold."

He walked over to her upholstered rocker-recliner and gingerly sat down. He smiled at her. "A cola sounds good."

She nodded. "I think I'll join you." She quickly filled a couple of glasses with ice and poured the colas over it. She returned to the living room, handed him his drink and sat on the sofa. Not wanting to get too comfortable, she remained perched on the edge of the couch, sipping the drink and enjoying her break.

"What do you want to discuss with me?" she finally asked, when Arthur appeared lost in his own thoughts.

He blinked and stared at her blankly before registering what she'd said. Then his face turned bright red.

"It's none of my business and I know that," he said. "The thing is, I've known you for five years and have greatly admired you. Not only as a person but as a consummate professional." His mouth curled into an amused smile. "I've been particularly grateful over the years for your protection of me from Brad's wrath."

"You knew what I was doing?" she asked, surprised.

"I may not be able to conduct myself smoothly around others, Rachel, but I'm not stupid."

"I'm very aware of that, Arthur."

"I actually admire Brad for what he's done with the company. He's made some astute business decisions over the years that not only are making him money now but will make even more in the future."

Now she was really puzzled. Why was he discussing Brad with her?

Nervously, he placed his glass on a coaster sitting next to his chair. He cleared his throat and said, "The thing is, I'm quite concerned about some of the decisions he's making in his personal life."

She started to reply, but he held up his hand. "Don't get me wrong. The very stubbornness and aggressiveness that are part of who the man is have helped him to overcome a great many obstacles.

However, I'm afraid those traits aren't as admirable when he runs roughshod over the people around him.''

She waited to reply until she was certain he'd completed what he wanted to say. When he remained silent, she spoke.

"Arthur, Brad may never tell you directly, but he considers you to be an integral part of the company, an absolute wizard with numbers. You've saved him—and the company—considerable money by studying how the company can best protect itself in today's market. I know he's not good at showing his gratitude.'' She smiled ruefully. "That's the reason he's so generous with his bonuses. It's the only way he knows to express gratitude.''

She could not believe she was defending the jerk.

Arthur looked at her, his bewilderment and confusion obvious. "But Rachel, I wasn't talking about *me*.''

It was her turn to be confused. "You weren't?''

"Of course not. It's *you* I've been worried about!''

Rachel gave her head a quick shake to clear her mind. She must have missed something during their interchange, although she could have sworn she had listened to every word he said.

"I'm afraid you're going to have to explain what you mean, Arthur. I'm not following you.''

He rubbed his forehead in obvious frustration. When he looked up, he said, "If I could only reduce what I'm trying to say to a mathematical equation, I would have no problem making myself clear.'' He grabbed his glass and took several swallows before returning it to the table.

"All right," he said. "Let me try to explain it this way. No. Let me ask you a question. How well do you know Brad Phillips?"

The headache she'd had since she woke was intensifying. Between lack of sleep, her marriage blowing up in her face—*from no fault of her own,* she wanted to state to one and all—and Arthur speaking in tongues, today obviously wasn't going to be one of her better days.

All right. She would play this his way. "I met Brad close to eight years ago, when he was first starting out. I thought you knew that."

He waved his hand impatiently. "I know how long you've *worked* for him, but how well do you *know* him?"

Good question. Obviously not as well as she'd thought...or hoped.

"Arthur," she said with strained patience, "Why don't you just tell me what you want to tell me, okay?"

He leaned back in his chair and took a deep breath. "I discovered quite by accident a few weeks ago that you have become romantically involved with him." He sounded more weary than disgusted.

"And—?" she asked, waiting for him to please get to the point. No wonder Brad lost patience with the man. Only a saint would be able to wait for him to explain his convoluted thought patterns.

"Well, after my interviews with him—and you,

too, of course—and the offer to join the company, I did a background check on him." He swallowed and adjusted his glasses.

"You did what?"

"I don't know how things are done in Texas, but back east we want to know about the person we're working for. I didn't want to accept employment only to discover later that the business was a front for illegal activities. Texas has a rather unsavory reputation for smuggling drugs and people and—" he waved his hand in the air "—things. I didn't want to be a part of any of that."

"Smuggling. I see. Well, I can understand how you might be concerned...being from the east and all."

He sighed with relief. "Thanks for being so understanding. I could find nothing illegal about the company but in checking Brad's records I discovered that he isn't who he says he is."

"He isn't? Then who is he?"

A look of distaste crossed his face. "I don't want to shock you with what I'm about to tell you, but I feel that it's in your best interest to know the truth about the man."

Rachel's fascination with the way this man's mind worked grew. "I see," she finally said, unable to think of anything else to say.

"His real name is Bradley J. Ogden but he has used many aliases, I'm sorry to say."

"Then Phillips isn't his real name?" she asked, filled with interest by this fascinating conversation.

"Well...I suppose it is now. It's his legal name.

He had it changed, which is suspicious in itself, don't you think?''

"Hmm," she replied as thoughtfully as possible.

"The worst part is his father has a long line of arrests, but very few convictions. At least until last year, when the authorities finally managed to put him behind bars!"

Her eyebrows lifted. "That *is* interesting," she said, wondering if Brad would want to know where his dad was…or if he cared. "All of this is of concern to you because I am currently romantically involved with him?"

He looked down at his hands clasped between his knees. "I would never want to see you hurt, Rachel. He might not mean to, but I'm very much afraid that if you choose to continue with your relationship, he'll hurt you in some way."

Too bad she hadn't received this warning last week, she thought. But then, last week she was still filled with fantasies about her marriage, her husband, a future family and their happy-ever-after life together.

Impulsively she reached over and patted his hands. "You are very kind to be so protective of me."

Her words didn't seem to help his dejected demeanor. "No, I'm not. It's not kindness at all!" He pulled his hands away from hers, straightened his spine and said, "I've been in love with you since soon after I joined the company, Rachel. I probably fell in love with you at that very first interview. You are everything I've ever wanted in a wife. I had hoped that someday you might come to feel the same way about me, but when you never responded to my notes, I decided that I was just fooling myself.''

Rachel caught her breath and stared at him in appalled shock. ''What exactly are you saying, Arthur? What notes are you talking about?''

His color flashed from pale to bright red and back to pale. His brow was beaded with moisture. ''I thought you might find it romantic if I left notes for you from your secret admirer. I figured you'd know who it was right away, but you never acknowledged them.''

Rachel jumped to her feet, staring at him in horror. ''Arthur, are you telling me that *you* are my stalker? Oh my God! I had no idea!''

He immediately looked offended. ''I am not a stalker, Rachel. All I did was leave messages telling you of my interest in you.''

''And you came into my apartment!''

''Just once. I swear. I'd decided to slip the note under your door—to be certain you received it—but when I got there, the door was ajar. The cleaning lady was in the bathroom with her radio on. I know it was stupid of me, but I wanted to surprise you. I just left the note on your dresser so the cleaning lady wouldn't accidentally toss it in the trash.''

''And you managed to scare me beyond anything I'd ever experienced! Arthur, do you realize what you've done?''

He blinked. ''What? What are you saying?''

''I went to the police thinking a stalker had come

into my apartment! I even went to North Carolina because—"

She stopped, realizing the results of what had happened. She fell onto the sofa and stared at him with renewed horror, her hands over her mouth.

His color was back to pasty white...she thought she much preferred his red stage. His eyes looked twice their normal size while he stared at her with panic. "I caused all of that? It was my notes to you? All the talk began about the two of you when you came back from North Carolina. You went because of me?"

"I went because I was scared, Arthur," she said slowly and clearly. "Your notes were becoming more and more explicit, as you may recall."

His face went red again. This time the color stayed. She wondered how long it could stay that way before he had a stroke. He looked away for a moment before returning his gaze toward her, although he refused to meet her eyes.

"I know I don't have a way with words. I've always known it. But I wanted you to know how I felt and how much I wanted to...wanted to..."

"We both know exactly what you wanted to do, Arthur. You made that quite clear."

"But I didn't mean to *scare* you! I didn't want you to think of me as some bumbling fool who didn't know what life was about."

She allowed her head to fall against the sofa. "You wanted to be considered sophisticated," she said dully, seeing the whole picture for the first time.

He nodded his head vigorously. "Exactly. Oh, Rachel, I am so sorry for frightening you. I had no idea you wouldn't immediately know the notes were from me.''

She wanted to scream at him. She wanted to kick and yell and throw a tantrum the likes of which Arthur Simmons had never before witnessed. Instead, she limited her reply to, ''The words *your secret admirer* really don't give much of a clue, Arthur.''

He looked woebegone. She saw moisture in his eyes but at the moment could find little sympathy for the man. Because of him she had actually jumped at the chance to marry Brad Phillips, thereby starting her down a long path—well, not all *that* long, actually—to pain, misery and suffering.

The pathetic weasel.

She sat there and stared at him malevolently. He met her stare with a nervous agitation that seemed to border on fear. Did he think she might attack him? Good. If her mother hadn't raised her to be a lady, she might very well do him bodily harm.

She closed her eyes in order to erase him from her thoughts. Her thoughts weren't having any of that and continued to bombard her with all kinds of realizations. One of them caused her eyes to flash open.

''You didn't come here to tell me about those notes. You came here to tell me about Brad's sordid past. Why?'' she demanded.

''I thought that was obvious. I love you. I want the best in life for you. I wouldn't have chosen Brad Phillips for you, but then I'm not very objective where you're concerned. I'm the first to admit it. I really thought I could make you happy. I realize now that I was deluding myself. Anyway, I thought that his aggressive behavior might have overwhelmed you, and that he might have taken advantage of you while you were in North Carolina." His voice rose slightly. "He's allowed all this talk to go on about you in the office and not once has he come to your defense. I was so angry when one of my accountants repeated something about you that I almost fired him on the spot."

He was working himself into a real snit, she decided. There was a lot of that going around these days, it seemed.

"Brad owes you a great deal more than to allow you to become the butt of office rumors."

Rachel closed her eyes again. "He didn't know about the rumors until yesterday."

"Oh. Then perhaps it's not too late for him to do the right thing."

"Which is?"

"Marry you, of course."

"Of course," she muttered. "Why didn't I think of that?"

Arthur stood and drew her to her feet. "I am so sorry that I had anything to do with causing you a moment's fright or pain. Can you ever forgive me?"

The man was distraught, that was obvious. She stared at him in blank despair. She'd made choices each step of the way, each time without having all the facts. She'd barged into Brad's safe haven and retreat, convinced she knew exactly what he needed and that she could provide it.

She looked into Arthur's kind but miserable eyes. She saw that he was truly contrite. Finally, she moved a step closer and placed her hands on his shoulders. "I forgive you, Arthur, but I suggest that you not write any more anonymous notes. And I would advise you not to discuss Brad's past with anyone else."

"Of course I won't! I don't divulge secrets, Rachel. You know that. I've never told another soul about Brad's dubious past. I believe the man has managed to redeem himself. Look where he is now."

Why did any of this matter to her, anyway? He'd fired her as a wife and as his assistant. If he hadn't, he might as well do so now. If he thought she would continue to work for him after all the horrible things he'd said to and about her, he was wrong.

She focused on the man in front of her. "Then let's keep all of this our secret, okay?"

He nodded solemnly. "I don't deserve your forgiveness, but thank you for it, anyway." He looked around the room uncertainly. "I need to go and let you get back to whatever it is you're doing," he said.

Before he stepped back she slipped her arms around his neck and fiercely hugged him. He didn't seem to know what to do with his hands but eventually placed them gently on her back.

That's the way Brad found them when he let himself into her apartment.

Chapter Twelve

Arthur leaped away from Rachel as though he'd touched an electric socket. So much for protecting her from their ogre of a boss. She, on the other hand, stayed where she was. She'd forgotten that she'd given Brad a key to her apartment. It had been more symbolic than practical, since there was no reason for him to be there without her.

She waited for him to launch into another round of accusations. At least he would have more cause today. If she wasn't already upset from Arthur's revelations on top of yesterday's painful scene, she might find it amusing that her suspicious husband had discovered her in the arms of another man.

Brad looked terrible. His eyes were swollen and bloodshot, his hair stuck out in several directions as though he'd forgotten to comb it after his shower and he was in need of a shave. Given his physical condition and his choice of clothes—where had he found them? she wondered—he could be mistaken for a homeless person.

He stood in the middle of the room and looked around him at the obvious signs of packing before he focused on Arthur. Brad looked bewildered by Arthur's presence.

"Uh…hi, Arthur. Sorry for bursting in like this," he said. He gave Rachel a quick glance before speaking to Arthur. "I guess I wasn't thinking about the possibility that Rachel might have company."

His tone was apologetic, which surprised both of them.

Arthur immediately stammered, "Oh! I'm the one who should apologize." He smiled nervously. "Dropping in unexpectedly this way. I'm sure you're both very busy." He'd begun to back to the door with each word until he was flat against it when he finished speaking. "So I'll…uh…I'll just, you know, be on my way," he added weakly, "and I'll, uh…see you Monday."

With that, he jerked the door open and practically ran out of the room.

The sound of the door slamming filled the silence left by Arthur's departure.

Rachel was not ready to face Brad. She was too angry, too hurt, too filled with misery to have to deal with him at the moment.

Too bad. He was here now, ready or not. From the

looks of him, he must have the granddaddy of all hangovers. She'd been around Brad when he wasn't feeling well. It had never been a pleasant experience even when she'd been capable of coping with him. Today was not one of those days.

He hadn't moved since Arthur had left and was growing paler by the moment. She nodded to the chair Arthur had vacated and said, "Sit down before you fall down. I'll make you some coffee."

Brad sat.

Rachel went into the kitchen, thankful she hadn't packed the coffeepot and supplies. She concentrated—or tried to—on measuring the coffee and water.

It really wasn't fair, she thought. He'd broken her heart, stomped all over her feelings for him, then had the nerve to show up on her doorstep looking like a waif. A hung-over waif, but adorable all the same. Damn him.

Her problem was that she knew him so well. Over the years she'd gotten to know his every mood, every expression, and at times could come close to reading his mind, which is why she'd been so unprepared for his crushing accusations yesterday. She'd never seen him like that before. She certainly never wanted to see him that way again.

Now that he was here and sober—suffering, but sober—she had to decide how to deal with the situation. She already knew he was ashamed of yesterday's behavior and today was contrite. But she couldn't pretend it had never happened.

She didn't know where to go from here. It was the
first time in all their time together that his anger and
distrust had been turned on her. Regardless of how
contrite he might be, she didn't think she could put
herself in a position where she'd be forced to deal
with another scene like that at some time in the future.

Rachel filled a glass with water, picked up a bottle
of aspirin tablets and took them to Brad. He was resting his head on the back of the chair with his eyes
closed. He opened them when she set the glass and
bottle on the table beside him.

''Thanks,'' he murmured, reaching for the pain re-
liever.

Rachel turned away without meeting his gaze. She
picked up her cold drink and finished it on her way
to the kitchen. That's when she remembered that she
had already packed all her dishes. Great. She dug
through three boxes before she found one of her large
cups.

After filling it with the extra strong coffee, she carried it into the living room. Brad stood and took the
cup from her. She turned and walked across the room
to sit on one of the wooden kitchen chairs.

Brad lowered himself into the chair again and carefully tasted the steaming brew. After a moment he
looked at her and said, ''Thank you for not throwing
me out of here.''

''Why are you here?''

He started to speak and stopped. He took another
sip of coffee and started to say something…and

stopped. Finally, he shrugged and said, "I wanted to stop you from leaving."

"I have no choice. I have to be out of the apartment by Monday." She looked away from him. She couldn't recall ever seeing him so subdued. In the old days, she would have found out what was bothering him and worked to find a solution.

Not this time.

"What are your plans?" he asked politely.

"They're still evolving."

They sat in silence while he drank his coffee. When his cup was empty, he placed it carefully on the table, then looked up and caught her in his intense gaze.

"What I did yesterday...what I said...all of it... was inexcusable." He rubbed his hand over his mouth and she heard the rasp of his chin whiskers rub against his palm. "I know that I acted like an insane man. I made a complete ass of myself." His eyes darkened. "There is no way I can tell you how sorry I am."

Rachel could think of nothing to say in reply. She was sure he spoke the truth.

Another silence lengthened. Brad got up and wandered over to the window, his hands in his pockets. She wondered if he knew how that particular pose emphasized the shape of his butt.

She used to have a difficult time not showing her reaction to him in his tight work jeans...and that was before she'd explored the taut muscles beneath them with her own body.

Not fair at all.

With his back to her, Brad said, "I don't remember much about yesterday. Mercifully. Because the things I do remember sicken me...the things I said to you...the way I spoke to you...to you, of all people."

"You said what you believed to be true."

"No," he said, shaking his head slowly. "I spoke aloud what I was afraid could be true."

"I see. You think I'm having an affair with Rich Harmon," she said in a neutral tone, ignoring her clenched stomach and the tears that kept surfacing.

He turned, removing his hands from his pockets as he did so. He grabbed the side of the window to steady himself.

"No," he said, his jaw stiff. "I do not think you are having an affair...with Harmon or anyone else."

"Then I don't understand what yesterday was all about," she managed to say.

He leaned against the wall as though he needed help to stand and studied her. She knew what he saw. A pale woman with no makeup, hair in a ponytail, wearing a dusty T-shirt and faded jeans.

"Have you ever wondered why, in all the years we've worked together, I never showed any personal interest in you? Never asked for a date? Never flirted with you?"

She thought about that. She'd been so busy hiding any hint of her fantasies about him while she was at work that she hadn't really noticed. "If I did," she finally said, "it was only a passing thought. With the hours you worked, you had no time for a social life."

"I mean later."

"I suppose I thought it was because you knew that office romances are fraught with potential problems."

He smiled for the first time since he'd arrived. "It's because you're the kind of woman who not only knows the meaning of the word fraught, but can use it in a sentence."

She frowned. He'd lost her on that one.

"I knew from the first day I met you that you were out of my league. You were polished, educated, came from a level of society I'd only viewed from a distance. You were the kind of classy lady destined to marry someone equally polished and educated, who moved in all the right circles. I would never let myself entertain the idea that you might think of me as anything other than your rather rough-edged boss."

Rachel stared at him, stunned by his words.

"You deserve someone so much better than me. I knew that when I hired you. I knew that when I married you. I knew better than to take advantage of your fears to convince you to marry me. But I did it anyway."

He pushed away from the wall and walked back to his chair. Seated, he said, "One of the things I remember from yesterday was you saying that I didn't trust you." He leaned forward and rested his elbows on his knees. "That isn't true. What I thought when I heard that you and Harmon had been seen having lunch in the park was that you had finally faced what a bad bargain you'd made by marrying me. Let's face it. Rich Harmon is much more in your class than I am."

Rachel didn't know whether to laugh or cry. How could he possibly think these things? All these years and she'd had no idea he had such a poor opinion of himself. Her thoughts were flying in all directions, reviewing everything he'd said yesterday through this new filter.

"I let my fear of losing you push me over the edge yesterday. I'd ask you to forgive me but I don't deserve your forgiveness. Anyone stupid enough not to realize he's been in love with you for the past eight years doesn't deserve you. Tell me what you want, Rachel. If you want a divorce, I won't stand in your way. If you feel you can no longer work with me, I'll deal with that as well."

So there it was. He'd come over today to ask forgiveness and to offer her freedom if that's what she wanted.

She let the tears go. "I don't want a divorce. I want to kill you for being so stupid. I want to kick you around the block several times. But no, I don't want to end our marriage."

He left his chair and sank down on his haunches next to her. "If you'll forgive me," he said, taking her hand with one of his, while he wiped a tear from her cheek with the other, "I promise you that I will never put either of us through this again. I promise never to doubt you, or be suspicious of you or demand explanations or refuse to listen to you." His voice broke. "If you'll forgive me, I'll be the best possible husband I can be."

She smiled through her tears. "That's good. For a minute I thought you were applying for sainthood."

He'd started to say something more but stopped at her words. "Does that mean there's a chance you'll forgive me?"

She stood, pulling him up as well. "If I say yes, will you go home and get some sleep? You look awful."

He slid his arms around her waist. "Only if you'll come home with me. I discovered I don't like sleeping without you."

She looked around the room and back to him. "All right. But I still have to be out of here by Monday."

He walked her to the door, his arm firmly around her waist. "You will be, if I have to bring one of my crews over here to do it!" He opened the door for her and when they were in the hall and the door secure, Brad turned to her and said, "By the way, what was Arthur doing here, if you don't mind my asking?"

She laughed and grabbed his hand. As they headed for the elevator, she said, "I would never have imagined Arthur in the role of Cupid, but wait until you hear what he told me."

Epilogue

Nine Years Later

"Mom?" Eight-year-old Casie, named after "Granddad" Casey, was busy helping Rachel clean the kitchen after a large Sunday meal.

"What, sweetie?" she asked absently, briskly wiping down the counter before starting the dishwasher.

"How did you and Daddy get together?"

"You've heard that story hundreds of times, Casie. He hired me to work for him soon after I graduated from college."

"That's not what I mean. I guess what I'm asking is, what made you decide to get married when you did if you'd worked for him for a long time?"

Rachel turned the switch on and the dishwasher

started purring into action. She tucked her daughter—
who looked mostly like her daddy, but with her
mother's eyes and hair—against her side. "I think
that's a great question. I bet your daddy can answer
it for you. Let's go see."

She already knew where she'd find him—stretched
out on their bed watching a football game on television. He'd used the excuse that he needed to lie down
with the boys because it was the only way he could
get five-year-old Brandon and two-year-old Benjamin
to take their naps without a fuss.

Brad had promoted Carl and Rich Harmon and a
couple of site managers, so he spent much less time
working than he once had. Rachel acted as a consul-
tant to Brad and continued to help with some of the
more difficult clients, but she seldom went into the
office.

She and Casie walked into the bedroom and sure
enough, both boys were sound asleep, one cuddled on
each side of Brad.

Casie went bouncing over to the bed and scrambled
onto it. Brad quickly put his finger over his mouth
and nodded to her brothers. She gave a little nod but
was too impatient to wait. In a loud whisper, she said,
"Mom said you would tell me what made you decide
to marry each other."

He'd been watching his daughter with indulgent
adoration, an expression he wore most of the time
when he was with their little ones. Rachel watched
Brad's eyes narrow slightly at his daughter's question.

"Mommy said to ask me, did she?" He kept his

voice soft, but the look he gave Rachel spoke volumes.

Casie nodded her head vigorously. "I've looked through the pictures taken at your wedding. You looked so happy together. It made me wonder why you waited to get married when you loved each other for so long."

"Hmm," he said. "Good question. Way back then I was so busy working that I didn't notice much around me. Then one day your mother and I had to go on a business trip and we needed to fly."

"Mommy hates to fly," Casie pointed out and rolled her eyes.

"That's right. So while we were flying, Mommy got really, really scared and she threw her arms around my neck and cried," he slipped into a falsetto voice, "'Save me, oh please save me.' That's when I truly looked at her for the first time, with my heart as well as my eyes. I thought, 'My, my, what a pretty lady you are. Where have you been all my life?' I decided that I would save her from everything scary in life and keep her safe here with me. And that's what I did. So you see, that's how it came about that your mother and I got married."

His eyes were filled with laughter when he glanced at Rachel and asked, "Isn't that right, pretty lady?"

She should have known he'd come up with a highly creative answer. "You're telling the story, not me," she replied, struggling not to laugh.

"So you saved her by marrying her and she wore that pretty dress and you got all dressed up, too, and had a beeoootiful wedding." Casie nodded to the small table that held their wedding picture album.

"Yep, that's what I did. I saved her, like a prince in one of your fairy tales."

Casie fell back on the bed and sighed a very large sigh of contentment. "And you lived happily ever after," she said with satisfaction.

Brad's eyes sent a heated message to Rachel, silently warning her that she would be paying for this much later that night.

"Yes, baby-girl, that's exactly what we're doing. We're living happily ever after."

*   *   *   *   *

Beloved author
JOAN ELLIOTT PICKART
introduces the next generation of MacAllisters in

The Baby Bet:
MACALLISTER'S GIFTS

with the following heartwarming romances:

On sale July 2002
THE ROYAL MACALLISTER
Silhouette Special Edition #1477
As the MacAllisters prepare for a royal wedding,
Alice "Trip" MacAllister meets her own Prince Charming.

On sale September 2002
PLAIN JANE MACALLISTER
Silhouette Desire #1462
A secret child stirs up trouble—and long-buried
passions—for Emily MacAllister when she is reunited
with her son's father, Dr. Mark Maxwell.

And look for the next exciting installment of
the MacAllister family saga, coming only to
Silhouette Special Edition in December 2002.

Don't miss these unforgettable romances...
available at your favorite retail outlet.

Silhouette®
Where love comes alive™

If you enjoyed what you just read,
then we've got an offer you can't resist!

Take 2 bestselling love stories FREE!

Plus get a FREE surprise gift!

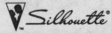

**Where royalty and romance
go hand in hand...**

The series continues in Silhouette Romance
with these unforgettable novels:

HER ROYAL HUSBAND
by Cara Colter
on sale July 2002 (SR #1600)

THE PRINCESS HAS AMNESIA!
by Patricia Thayer
on sale August 2002 (SR #1606)

SEARCHING FOR HER PRINCE
by Karen Rose Smith
on sale September 2002 (SR #1612)

And look for more Crown and Glory stories in
SILHOUETTE DESIRE starting in October 2002!

Available at your favorite retail outlet.

Where love comes alive™

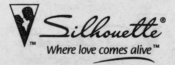

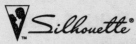

COMING NEXT MONTH

#1477 THE ROYAL MacALLISTER—Joan Elliott Pickart
The Baby Bet: The MacAllister Family
Independent-minded Alice "Trip" MacAllister and ravishing royal
Brent Bardow, cousin of the Prince of Wilshire, were unexpectedly in
love. Problem was, a once-burned Brent was wary of women with
"secret agendas." But, when Brent discovered that Alice, too, had her
own agenda, would he flee in anger…or help turn Alice's dreams
into reality?

#1478 WHITE DOVE'S PROMISE—Stella Bagwell
The Coltons: Commanche Blood
Kerry WindWalker's precious baby girl had gone missing, and
only Jared Colton could save her. The former town bad boy was
proclaimed a hero—but all he wanted as a reward was Kerry. Would
spending time with the beautiful single mom and her adorable tot
transform this rugged rescuer into a committed family man?

#1479 THE BEST MAN'S PLAN—Gina Wilkins
It was only make-believe, right? Small-town shopkeeper
Grace Pennington and millionaire businessman Bryan Falcon
were just *pretending* to be in love so the ever-hungry tabloids
would leave Bryan alone. But then the two shared a sizzling night
of passion, and their secret scheme turned into a real-life romance!

#1480 THE McCAFFERTYS: SLADE—Lisa Jackson
The McCaffertys
Slade McCafferty was the black sheep of his family—and the man
who once shattered lawyer Jamie Parson's young heart. But then
Jamie returned to her hometown for work, and the spark between the
polished attorney and the rugged rogue ignited into fiery desire.
Would a shocking injury resolve past hurts…and make way for a
heartfelt declaration?

#1481 MAD ENOUGH TO MARRY—Christie Ridgway
Stood up…on prom night! Elena O'Brien, who grew up on the wrong
side of the tracks, had never forgotten—or forgiven—rich boy Logan
Chase. Eleven years later, Elena wound up living under one roof with
Logan, and new desires began to simmer. Then another prom night
arrived, and Logan finally had a chance to
prove his true love for his old flame….

#1482 HIS PRIVATE NURSE—Arlene James
A suspicious fall had landed sexy Royce Lawler in the hospital and
in the care of pretty nurse Merrily Gage. And when it was time to go
home Royce offered Merrily the position of his private nurse—a job
she happily accepted, never realizing that caring for her handsome
patient would throw both her heart and her life in danger.

SSECNM0602

SPECIAL EDITION